Books by Peter Dickinson

THE WEATHERMONGER

HEARTSEASE

THE DEVIL'S CHILDREN

EMMA TUPPER'S DIARY

EMMA
TUPPER'S
DIARY

EMMA
TUPPER'S
DIARY

Peter Dickinson

Illustrated by David Omar White

An Atlantic Monthly Press Book
Little, Brown and Company
BOSTON   TORONTO

ATLANTIC–LITTLE, BROWN BOOKS
ARE PUBLISHED BY
LITTLE, BROWN AND COMPANY
IN ASSOCIATION WITH
THE ATLANTIC MONTHLY PRESS

PRINTED IN THE UNITED STATES OF AMERICA

EMMA
TUPPER'S
DIARY

1

"Yesterday was surprising," wrote Emma Tupper. She stared out of her bedroom window and rattled her pen across her upper teeth. The loch lay so still in the early morning stillness that you might have skated on it. Then, beyond the water, a mountain rose, dark cliffs at the bottom, and above them mottled yellow and brown and purple — patches of grass and heather, Emma thought. The smooth sweep of the crest was spoiled by a funny little bobble. Dulled last night by her long journey, she hadn't realized quite how beautiful it all was; but she decided not to write about it now and to save it up for a day when nothing

much happened. Yesterday had been surprising enough for one day's entry.

Emma had always awakened far too early for any sane household. Ever since she could remember there had been at least two hours to mooch away before breakfast, but now she was going to use the time. She was going to write a better holiday diary than Sarah Davidson, who was spending her holidays in the Algarve, in Portugal. Sarah thought she would win the School Prize with her diary. Huh!

"Yesterday was surprising," Emma read. Yes, it was. She started to write quickly in her large but tidy script. "I had a headache when the train got to Waverley Station in Edinburgh, and I couldn't see anyone to meet me. But then I heard the loudspeakers calling my name."

". . . Will Miss Emma Tupper, passenger on the 14–19 train from King's Cross, please come to the Stationmaster's Office?"

She must have heard it three times before she noticed it, booming away amid the roof girders while the flood of other passengers rushed past her and she searched among the blank backs for a face that looked as if it might be coming to meet her. Two boys, a girl, some sort of looker-after person called Miss Newcombe. . . . Then she heard her own name shouted up in the girders and listened to the message properly next time around.

A porter was pulling past her with a trolley covered with racing pigeons crowded into woven hampers. The birds

4

looked beady-eyed but placid — *they* knew what was happening; Emma didn't.

"Please, where's the Stationmaster's Office?" she said to the man.

He began to point and explain, then noticed her heavy old suitcase.

"OK," he said, picking it up and stowing it behind the pigeons. "I'll show you. I'll be going most of the way, y'see."

Emma was disappointed that he didn't sound particularly Scottish, but she gave him a shilling when he put the case down on the floor of the Stationmaster's Office. This wasn't a room — more like a passage with several doors opening off it, one of which said ENQUIRIES. RING AND WAIT. Emma rang, a glass partition beside the door shot up; a Jamaican's face appeared and said, "Yes. Can I help you, please?"

"I'm Emma Tupper. The loudspeaker was calling for me."

"Fine fine fine," said the man. "Your friend's here, miss."

"Thank you so much, Simon," said a slow, soft voice. It sounded half awake, as though somebody had just brought it a cup of early morning tea. The door beside the partition opened and out walked a young woman. Emma forgot her headache and stared. It was impossible to believe that she could be in the same room — between these dingy walls — with anyone so beautiful. The woman didn't seem to mind being stared at, or even to notice.

"Hello," she said. "Are you Emma? I'm Poop Newcombe. Now the first thing is . . . he said it was very im-

5

portant . . . I've got a letter for you . . . I think. Here."

She spoke in a dreamy way, as though she could never be sure what the next word was going to be. She was blond, not very tall, wearing a neat tweed suit. Her skin looked so soft that you'd have thought one touch would bruise it, or at least spoil it in the way a touch spoils the powdery freshness of an iris stalk. Her eyes were very dark blue, and she kept them very wide open. As she gave Emma the letter she smiled as though she were thinking about something else.

The envelope was thick and creamy, with no writing on it. The paper inside crackled expensively as she unfolded it, and bore at the top an elaborate printed scroll containing the words "McAndrew's Infallible Liniment for the Scalp"; luxuriant swags of hair fringed the scroll. After all this the actual message seemed very short and scrawled:

> *Dear Cousin Emma,*
>   *Don't let Poop go into any shops. Bring her straight back here. Important.*
>   *R. McAndrew.*

"Is R. McAndrew Roderick?" said Emma.

Miss Newcombe turned from where she had been looking at her reflection in the glass covering a map of Scotland.

"Yes," she said, "but you needn't worry. He makes jokes . . . and things. Shall we go? Oh, Simon . . ."

The dark head appeared smiling at the partition.

"Yes, miss?"

"What on earth shall we do about this?"

She frowned at Emma's suitcase as though it were a quite new kind of problem.

6

"No trouble, miss," said Simon. He nipped away, and Emma heard the chittering dial of the telephone. Almost at once another porter appeared and picked up the suitcase.

"Oh, how lucky," said Miss Newcombe. "I wonder if he can find us a taxi, and then we can go shopping."

The porter, a weedy and whiskery old man, tottered quickly through the bustle of travelers, as though he were determined to show Miss Newcombe that he was still as spry as a youngster. An army officer with red tabs on his shoulders was waiting for a taxi at the rank. Miss Newcombe frowned into her handbag.

"I don't seem to have any money, Emma," she said. Emma was tipping the porter as a taxi appeared, so she didn't see quite how it happened that the officer should be holding the door to let Miss Newcombe climb in, though it was really his taxi. The driver stowed Emma's suitcase, climbed into his seat, and said "Where to, ma'am?"

"Oh," said Miss Newcombe. "That lovely big shop . . . what's its name?"

"Forsyths? Or Jenners?" said the driver.

"That's right," said Miss Newcombe happily. The driver shrugged and drove off.

"Please," said Emma. "I mean, I'm sorry. I mean I've got a headache. Are the shops important? Where are the others? I thought . . ."

"Have you really got a headache?" said Miss Newcombe.

"Yes. I took a Disprin in the train, but it doesn't seem to be working."

Miss Newcombe looked disappointed.

"Poor darling," she said. "I'll take you to the office — they're all there, and they'll know what to do. They'd have come to meet you, only something's happened to the company. I'm sorry, driver, we've changed our minds. Could you take us to . . . to . . . here it is. . . ."

She pulled out of her handbag another sheet of the expensive paper and held it so that Emma could read the words on the back while she read the address on the front. The words on the back were upside down, but they were in the same big scrawl as her letter, and easy to read. "Taxi to Waverley Station. Go to STATIONMASTER'S OFFICE. Find SIMON. Ask him to broadcast message for EMMA TUPPER, on 14–19 from King's Cross. GIVE HER MY LETTER! Don't try and find the platform — you'll get lost. DON'T GO SHOPPING — *There isn't time!!*"

"How old are they all?" said Emma. "Mummy wasn't sure in her letter."

"Who, darling?"

"The McAndrews."

"I'm twenty-six," said Miss Newcombe, "and Andy's four years younger than me, and Finn's four years younger than him, and Roddy's four years younger than her. I *hate* arithmetic, but if *you* don't mind . . ."

"Is Finn Fiona?"

"Yes, darling."

"So she's eighteen?"

"I expect so. Did you work it out? She *looks* eighteen . . . usually."

Emma was disappointed. The gap between eighteen and her own fourteen was probably too big for easy friendship; she would have to fall back on Cousin Roderick, who wrote strange letters which were probably practical jokes. Except that his note to Miss Newcombe had told her not to go

8

shopping . . . though how she was going to do that without any money . . .

"Hurrah," said Miss Newcombe suddenly. "Here we are. McAndrew's Infallible Liniment — that's it. You *are* clever. Well done."

The last five words were spoken to the driver, who grinned as though they were the biggest tip he'd ever been given. He jumped out to hold the door for her, only to find that it was already being opened by a twisted little man who was wearing shiny black riding boots, breeches, a blue jacket with silver buttons, and a peaked cap.

"Oh, thank you, Andy," said Miss Newcombe. "Have you got something to pay the driver with? He drove terribly well."

"I'll see to it, Miss Poop. The others have just about finished their talk. Will you and the young lady be waiting in the car?"

(*Actually, what the little man said was more like "I'll see tae ut, Miss Poop. Ta ithers hae juist aboot feeneeshed thair tack. Wiull ye an ta young leddy be wetting in ta carr?" Emma tried many times to get a few sentences of the shushing, lilting West Highland accent into her diary, but they never looked right.*)

At that moment a small crowd burst from the door of McAndrew's Infallible Liniment. It consisted of only four people but it had all the jostling and confusion of larger crowds until it sorted itself out; then three of the people lined up on the pavement to shake hands with the fourth — a fattish, dapper man who bowed as he took each hand. He looked very worried.

"Good-bye, Mr. Andrew," he said to the dark, fierce,

handsome young man. "I'm afraid this has been an unlucky visit."

"Good-bye, Mr. Crowe," said the young man. "I'll write to my father, but you know what he's like about letters."

"Good-bye, Mr. Crowe," said the thin girl with the pale long face and marvelous long red-orange hair. "Give my love to your wife."

"Good-bye, Old Crow," said the dark boy — square-headed, black-eyed, leaning forward as though he wanted to punch Mr. Crowe instead of shaking hands with him. "You'll have to form a new political party and make yourself prime minister and change the law."

Mr. Crowe smiled at last through his worry.

"Hi, Poop," said the young man. "Did you find her? Are you sure she's the right one?"

"I *think* so," said Miss Newcombe, staring dazedly at Emma.

"Well, are you the right one?" said the young man.

"I'm Emma Tupper." She made the words sound as stodgy as she could.

"Great," said the young man, grinning like a bandit. "I'm Andy, and I'm an engineer. This is Finn, and she's an artist. This is Roddy, and he's a nuisance."

"You're still learning to be an engineer," said Roddy. "I know how to be a nuisance."

"Let's go, then," said Andy.

He swung around and led the way to a huge Jaguar sedan parked a few yards down the street; the other Andy was wrestling Emma's suitcase into its trunk. Roddy stayed for a moment where he was, raised his black eyebrows slightly, and glanced sideways at Miss Newcombe's slim back. Emma shook her head and he gave her a thumbs-up sign. Then they followed the rest of the family into the plushy, leather-smelling interior of the Jaguar, Andy shut the doors, and the car sighed away from the curb, slow as a hearse, with the little old Andy driving.

"Is it far?" said Emma.

"About two hundred miles," said Finn.

"Don't worry," said Roddy, as a boy on a bicycle overtook them. "Andy and Poop'll drive most of the way. Andy Coaches only drives to keep Old Crow happy."

"Is everybody called Andy?" said Emma.

"All the McAndrews who live around the loch call their eldest son Andrew," said Finn. "You tell them apart by adding their job, or the place they live, as a sort of surname. Our Andy's called Andy Big House; Andy Coaches' father looked after the coach house in Grandfather's time, and so on."

"Our Cousin Emma's a good guesser," said Roddy. He lowered his voice and added, "Can you guess why Poop's called Poop?"

"Poop Newcombe," whispered Finn, as though she were giving Emma a hint. Hearing the name spoken in full again took Emma back to the moment when Miss Newcombe had first floated into Simon's office, wide-eyed and wonderful. The very first words she'd spoken had had a funny ring about them — "Hello. Are you Emma? I'm Poop Newcombe." That was wrong. It should have been . . . been Newcombe Poop? No . . .

"Nincompoop," whispered Emma.

Roddy whistled. As if that had been a signal, the car stopped and the two Andys changed places on the front seat, with Miss Newcombe between them. Then the upholstery was pressing against Emma's back as the big car accel-

11

erated away, faster and faster, until they were breaking the speed limit twice over.

"Nothing's going to keep Old Crow happy any longer, I suppose," said Roddy suddenly.

"Is something wrong?" said Emma. She knew something was wrong, of course, but it was difficult to ask.

"What about it, Andy?" said Finn.

"The poor girl's not going to hear about anything else for days," called Andy over his shoulder. "You'd better tell her."

Finn sighed and stared out of the window at the hurtling suburbs. By craning up and sideways Emma could see that the speedometer stood at 80 mph.

"Don't worry," said Roddy. "Andy Coaches keeps an eye out for the police. He's a whizz at that. He can smell 'em round a blind corner. Now, this follicle food. You know our grandfather — he was your great-grandfather, I suppose — was an inventor?"

"Yes, he invented a magnet for getting bits of iron out of people's eyes."

"That's his *famous* invention, but he invented lots of other things, all sorts of different things. We've still got his submarine in one of the boathouses, for instance, because he wanted to explore the loch to see if there was a monster in it. But the best thing he did . . ."

"You mean the best thing for people who haven't got bits of iron in their eyes," interrupted Finn.

"Shut up. The best thing he did was to invent this scalp lotion for his father-in-law, who looked like a mad scientist in a comic."

"No he didn't," said Finn. "He looked like a middle-aged man in an insurance advertisement. Mad scientists are bald all over. Great-grandfather Hamilton was just going bald, and he minded, so Grandfather invented a scalp lotion for him — McAndrew's Universal Liniment."

"And it worked?" said Emma.

"Not *exactly*," said Finn, "but a lot of people must have found it kind of comforting, because we always managed to sell quite a bit —"

"Except they kept changing the law," shouted Roddy. "First of all they stopped us saying it *cures* baldness —"

"That was ages ago," said Finn.

"And now we're not even allowed to say it *helps*. Cousin Emma, you have come to spend your holidays with a gang of paupers."

"I'm sorry," said Emma. The big car slowed where two lorries were overtaking each other along the dual highway. Andy let the hood nose right in under the tailboard of the outer one and pressed his fist on the horn button. It must have been a special sort of horn — the outrageous blare of it made talk impossible even in the back of the Jaguar, where most of the other traffic noises had been no more than a gentle drumming. Emma sat rigid, prickling with fear. This car didn't feel as though it belonged to a gang of paupers, she thought. Nor did a submarine in the boathouse — *one* of the boathouses. A crevasse opened at last between the outer lorry and the central crash barrier. Andy edged through. In a minute the speedometer stood at just under 100 mph.

"So Mr. Crowe had to tell us the company was in a bad way," said Finn. "We always have a shareholders meeting on the first day of the holidays, because we're all in Edinburgh about then anyway. It's a nuisance, Father being away."

"He'd only tell us to sort it out ourselves," shouted Roddy. "I've got a good mind to call an Extraordinary General Meeting. That'd make him take it seriously."

"Poor Cousin Emma," said Finn. "Father gave us the liniment company, so Mr. Crowe and Andy and I are directors, but Roddy can't be one till he's eighteen. Father and Roddy are the shareholders, but Father's never there. He doesn't like to be bothered, and I expect you don't either. Let's give it a rest, Roddy."

"I expect it's something to do with taxes," said Emma. "You being directors, I mean."

"That's what Father *says*," said Roddy.

"He also says it's educational," said Finn.

"But really he doesn't like to be bothered," they both said together.

"Now Cousin Emma can tell us what she's doing, foisting herself off on us for the whole holidays," said Roddy.

So Emma explained. As she did so she could see her father sitting in his tin-roofed office in far Botswana, trying to coax suspicious Africans to sow better strains of seed, while her mother stumped about in the heat and dust and told everybody, loud-voiced, how wrongly they were doing everything. She explained about the argument whether she should go to one of the schools in Botswana, as her father wanted, or a private school for white girls only in South Africa, as her mother wanted. And then the astonishing scholarship offered by this English school.

"But it costs too much for me to go home for the holidays," she said. "At Easter I stayed with my uncle, Daddy's brother, in Dorset, but he makes his living running a trailer camp and he's too busy in the summer to cope with

14

me. But Daddy went to a conference where he met your father, and they settled for me to come to you. I've got money to pay for my ticket to Dorset if it doesn't work."

"The English are a careful people," said Finn, laughing.

"Let's play The Game," said Roddy suddenly. So they taught Emma a complicated family game, guessing words by guessing at the letters in them. After three or four goes in which she did badly, Emma thought hard about it and worked out a system which meant you were almost bound to win. Roddy said it was cheating. Finn laughed and suggested a change in the rules. They played that way until Emma found a system for that, too. Roddy was just becoming furious when the car stopped.

Emma got out with the others and stared at the astounding view, a loch between gaunt hills, and not a house anywhere. The McAndrews lined up by the side of the road with their backs to the loch. "One, two, three, go," said Miss Newcombe, and they started to climb the hill. It was obviously a race, and Roddy was obviously going to win, so fiercely did he scramble and stride. Andy would be next, going quickly and steadily, and Finn was barely more than walking. Roddy reached a single big rock about two hundred yards up, shouted, and turned. He came down much more carefully than he'd climbed. Andy was second at the rock, shouted too, and came down at almost the same pace that he'd gone up — Emma saw that he might just about catch Roddy before they reached the road. It seemed ages after that before Finn touched the rock, shouted and turned; then she was coming down almost as if she were falling, in huge, sure-footed leaps, with her long orange hair streaming behind her in the wind of her coming. She gave a wild call as she passed Andy a few yards above the tarmac, but Roddy was on the road before her.

"Nine all," said Roddy exultantly. "Three more goes and I'll catch Andy."

"It started as a way of stopping car sickness," said Finn to Emma. "It was Father's idea. So we always did it on the first day of the holidays. It means term's over, you see."

"And that means we'll have to go on doing it till Roddy leaves school," said Andy. "Tradition can be a terrible taskmaster."

His lean, hard face looked quite cool, though not as cool as Finn's, who had allowed gravity to run most of her race for her. But Roddy was still sweating and panting, which Emma thought odd, considering how carefully he'd come down, though he must have nearly exhausted himself reaching the rock.

"Shall I drive now?" said Miss Newcombe.

"Right," said Andy. "Everybody in? Do you want to sit in front, Cousin Emma?"

Emma doubted if it mattered where she sat, as Miss Newcombe would probably drive them all in a vague swoop over the next cliff, but she got in on the outside of the front seat. Andy was already in the middle, adjusting the driving mirror so that he and not Miss Newcombe could see out of the back window. Once more the big engine took the car sighingly away.

In fact Miss Newcombe drove beautifully, almost as fast as Andy but without any of his sense of ferocious bustle. The road was much steeper and bendier, curving around shoulders of mountains or wriggling along steep valleys carved out by some frothy river, but she coaxed the miles away between the beautiful bare hills — not really bare like Botswana, but almost as much of a desert, with a few sheep nosing for grass in the acres of unnourishing heather. When at last they came to savage Glencoe, Andy told Emma the whole story from beginning to end, giving everybody's name as though he knew them himself and making it all sound as though it still mattered, every burned roof and every slaughtered child. At Ballachulish Ferry, Roddy introduced Emma by name to all the crewmen, saying that she was his cousin from Africa, and they shook hands with her and welcomed her to the Highlands. She sat in the back of the car again after that, and Andy drove. A gray, wet fog now covered the hills, so she never saw Ben Nevis, and after Fort William she slept. So it was another surprise to wake up and see the sea on their left, full of little rocky islands, and the sun slanting across them, and bigger islands far out across the water; and to realize that the low hills here were mostly dunes of the same sand as the shore; and then to turn inland to where the much bigger hills reared up, hills which must be rock to make them stand so tall and steep; to wind for miles along a road no wider than a cart track, with grass growing down the middle; to dip through a little wood of twisted oaks and come out right on the edge of water, where the road ran beside a lake not half a mile wide but piercing further and further into the hills as they saw fresh reaches around every bend; and at last to climb out of the car, yawning slightly but headachy no more, in front of the McAndrews' house.

The house itself was as much of a surprise as anything, because it was a bungalow with a verandah running down the front, like any South African farmhouse with its *stoep;*

except that this bungalow seemed almost a hundred yards long, and only the road lay between it and the black rocks at the water's edge.

A stout woman, gray-haired and gray-faced, was waiting at the top of the steps up to the verandah.

"Mary, this is my Cousin Emma," said Andy. "Mary looks after us, Emma, and sees that we don't starve."

"Come you in, Miss Emma," said Mary in an accent like Andy Coaches'. "It will be fine to have a sane body biding in the house again."

2

*"Yesterday was interesting some of the time
and ordinary some of the time," wrote Emma.
Outside her window the loch fidgeted under a
driving westerly; slanting gray shafts of rain
marched across it, but even between them she
couldn't see the far shore. She had been awakened in the night by the calls of wildcats, and
then had heard the first swishings of the storm.
She wrote the word "wildcat" on the last sheet of
her diary, to remind her to try and see one,
though Roddy said he never had, though he'd
hunted and hunted. But rare wild animals were
just what she wanted.*

*She looked out of the window again and saw
how the stream beyond the house was roaring*

*under the little timber bridge, pushing a stain of
mud-colored water out into the dark loch. Emma
would like to have described all that — her
teacher, Miss Sturmer, always gave good marks
for scenic description — but too much had happened yesterday, so it would have to wait. She
wondered whether Sarah Davidson had done anything as interesting as arguing what to use a loch
and a mountain for, or working out a scheme to
diddle a TV company, or trying to make an
eighty-year-old submarine work.*

The McAndrews ate in a room which at first sight had
given Emma a thrill of horror almost worse than the tiger
skins that hung in the paneled hall. So many beautiful animals had died in order that their polished horns should jut
from these walls — kudu and impala and gazelle, and worst
of all an Arabian oryx — and every one of them shot by her
own great-grandfather. She thought it wouldn't be polite
to tell her hosts how wicked the slaughter had been, how
few tigers there were left in the world — and even fewer
oryxes; but at supper her first night she couldn't keep her
eyes off the trophies.

By breakfast next day, however, she was growing used to
them. Tigers, she argued to herself, had been a pest in
great-grandfather's time, and there were probably even
quite a number of oryxes before the Arab princes started
shooting them with machine guns out of jeeps; perhaps
they could spare one, then. The idea was half comforting.

The McAndrews believed in breakfast. "So if we don't
want to come back to lunch we won't die of hunger," as
Roddy said when he got up to help himself to more scram-

bled eggs. On the sideboard there was also porridge and cream, fresh mackerel, bacon, kidneys, grilled tomatoes, brown whole-meal bread baked in the house, butter from the farm, marmalade from Oxford, tea and coffee and milk and Coca Cola. Doing justice to all this stilled even the McAndrews' tongues, at times.

In one silence Emma, who had been looking across the still loch to where the mountain basked placid in the sunlight, said, "What's that funny little bobble up there?"

Finn came around the table to peer along her pointing arm.

"That's Darwin's Pimple," she said. "It's a cairn, a sort of monument made by piling stones together. Grandfather quarreled with Darwin — not about evolution, about something else — but he quarreled with everybody. A long time after Darwin died he changed his mind and built a cairn to him. He even got Mary's great-aunt to put a curse on anyone who moved it. She was gifted with the gifts, you see. Mother wanted to move it because she said it looks like a pimple and spoils the line of the hill, but Father said we couldn't afford to offend Mary by doubting her great-aunt's gifts and curses."

"Does all that belong to you, then?" said Emma.

"Oh, yes, but no one else wants it. It isn't any use. There's forty acres of fertile land for the farm, and a few big patches on this side of the loch which Father has planted with conifers, but nothing except heather will grow on that side at all."

"My mother's brother, the one I was telling you about," said Emma. "He has a farm in Dorset. His biggest crop is trailers, which will grow on the worst soil on the farm, he says."

21

"Ugh," said all the McAndrews together.

"I know they're hideous," said Emma. "But you can hide them. He keeps his in a pinewood, and the people who come there like it better than the sites in open fields. If you put caravans in that oak wood we drove through you wouldn't have to build a road and they wouldn't have to come to and fro past you, which is the worst thing about my uncle's farm. You could arrange things so that you never saw people up here except when they were boating, and you could rent the boats to them for that. It's all so beautiful, and it's a waste only you being able to see it."

"You lack the aristocratic outlook, Cousin Emma," said Andy. "Of course only we should be able to see it."

He had his mouth full of kidney, but he managed the rebuke very aristocratically indeed.

"Cousin Emma has something," said Roddy. "The company ought to . . . what's the word?"

"Diversify," said Finn.

"We could get Old Crow to fiddle with the liniment and sell it as a sun lotion to the tourists," said Roddy.

"And have them going back to Glasgow with hair all over them?" asked Finn.

Andy sighed, grown-uply patient.

"They wouldn't come," he said. "What they want is the sea. Why should they come inland once they've reached the coast?"

"The coast's so crowded," said Finn.

"It rains less there," said Roddy.

"But if people knew it was here," said Emma. "There's always people who want to be a bit different, and if they knew how beautiful it was . . ."

"There's other lochs just as beautiful," said Finn. "Why should they choose this one? What's so special about it?"

"Hello," said Miss Newcombe's sleepy voice from the door. "Am I too late?"

She was barefooted and wore an ivory-colored quilted dressing gown. There was sleepy-dust in the corner of her eyes, and she hadn't brushed her hair or put on any make-up, but Emma adored her all over again looking like that, a sleepy goddess. Mary came running from the kitchen at the sound of her voice.

"There's fresh yoghurt made, Miss Poop," she said, plonking a big bowl on the sideboard. "I kept it back till you woke, so that it would not all be gobbled up by these bigmouths. Och, Miss Emma, I was forgetting you — have you space for some yoghurt now?"

"No thank you," said Emma, a truthful girl.

"What were you talking about?" said Miss Newcombe. "Somebody being beautiful?"

"Some*thing* being beautiful," said Roddy.

"Oh," said Miss Newcombe in a disappointed voice.

"We were arguing about how we could make our loch seem more interesting than other lochs," said Finn.

"But it's got the creature, hasn't it, Mary?" said Miss Newcombe.

"Indeed it has," said Mary.

Roddy looked as though the whole glorious day had been suddenly spoiled.

"Something *real!*" he shouted. "Something to make the beastly tourists come here!"

"Creature?" said Emma. "Do you mean a monster?"

Andy laughed.

"Oh yes, we've got one of those," he said. "It's made of rafts of weed which get carried up from the bottom by gases from decaying stuff underneath them. They make black hummocks, quite long sometimes, so that you see several things in line that might be the humps of a sea serpent, and then the gas gets out and they sink again. That's what all the monsters really are — Loch Ness and Loch Morar as well as ours. How long since anybody saw its head, Mary? Mouth, eyes, teeth?"

"Och, you'll not see them and live," said Mary placidly. "But there was poachers came up from Glasgow when you were in your cradle, Master Andy — an ignorant class of men, as everybody knows there's no fish worth poaching in our loch. But they brought two boats by night, and nets, and by morning both boats were overturned and three of the men vanished. Those were the last poachers I heard of coming this way."

"And the first," said Roddy. "Everyone knows there's no fish worth poaching. Hey!"

Mary had walked around behind his chair while he was talking, and now biffed him hard on the ear with her open palm; then she nodded to Emma and walked out smiling. Roddy rubbed his ear and went on eating his toast.

"Even if there's only a *story* about a monster . . ." said Emma. "I mean, there's only a story about Loch Ness."

"That one's had two hundred years to spread," said Andy.

"But things happen so much faster now," said Emma. "I mean, if only you could get your story on television . . ."

"Cousin Emma," said Andy, lordly and handsome, "you have only just reached civilization after a formative child-hood in the desert. Understandably you are besotted by the television set. But you will later learn that it cannot do everything — in particular it cannot make one stretch of water which might have a monster in it look more interesting than another stretch of water which might not."

"He's the expert," said Roddy. "His girl's in the Glasgow studios."

"You're out of date, you nasty little tattler," said Andy with sudden sharpness.

"Come on, Cousin Emma," said Finn. "You've had all the ideas. Don't let him shoot you down."

Something about her tone and glance told Emma that it mattered, though she couldn't guess how. She thought hard.

"Yes, I see," she said. "That means . . . that means you've got to have something you can actually see in the water. If you had a movie camera . . ."

"If!" whooped Roddy. "Once Finn's got going the whole valley rattles with camera shutters from dawn to dusk. She once spent three whole days photographing one stone on the shore."

"*And* I got one of the pictures into an exhibition," said Finn. "Go on, Cousin Emma."

"Well, you might be able to wait for one of these rafts to come up, and photograph it, and if it looked real enough you'd have something to show the television people, and if —"

"My dear Cousin Emma," said Andy, still angry enough to sound sneering rather than teasing, "I doubt if these blobs come to the surface twice in a whole year, and always in different places. You'd have to be within thirty yards of one, camera loaded and ready, for anything to show at all. Fat chance!"

"Don't let's leave it to nature, then," said Finn. "Let's do the faking ourselves."

Andy started to say something squelching, stopped, snatched a sugar lump from the bowl, threw it in the air and caught it in his mouth.

"Right," he said when he'd finished crunching it up. "We'll start from there. It's an idiot idea, but it's an excuse to see if Anna will still go. If she will, we'll try putting a superstructure on her, a monster's head and neck, and —"

"It'll have to be pretty strong," said Roddy. "You'll need to get Anna out of sight under the water, and when she surfaces she's got to go fast enough to show a wake behind the neck. I read a book about Loch Ness last term and much the best picture of *their* monster, the only one that looks like anything at all, has a wake behind. That means you can see it's moving."

"Can do," said Andy. "We'll use the fiber glass I bought for the Lotus. Laminate it thick enough onto a wire skeleton and it'll do. There'll be a bit of a problem fastening it to Anna, but it ought to be possible. Anything will do for the tail — it's only got to show in one or two places. We could fill a couple of tractor inner tubes with water until they were barely buoyant and trail them behind Anna —"

"I thought her name was *Emma*," said Miss Newcombe. "In fact I'm almost sure it was. You won't let them do anything you don't like, will you, darling? They can be very wild."

"Anna Di Ommany!" shouted Roddy.

"No," said Miss Newcombe. "Emma something."

"It's all right," said Emma. "They're not talking about me. I think it's the submarine, isn't it?"

Finn nodded.

"Victorian scientists had a wild time," said Andy. "They could study anything they wanted and still have time to keep up with the arts. Grandfather experimented and worked in half a dozen different fields, but he still read Homer in Greek while he was waiting for experiments to work. He called his sub *Anadyomene,* which means 'coming up from the waves' — you remember that Botticelli picture of Venus wafting ashore in a seashell with —"

"She looks a bit like Poop," said Finn.

"Does she?" said Miss Newcombe with sudden interest.

"Botticelli's *Venus Anadyomene,* yes," said Andy. "Our *Anadyomene,* no. Anna's an ugly old sow, but she works."

"Not at all like Poop, then," said Roddy.

"Father had her out in 1953 to celebrate the Coronation," said Andy. "I can just remember. He had to do *something,* as Clan Chief, so he held a Clan Muster here. It was his excuse for not going to London. Mother was furious."

"You can't remember that part," said Finn. "You were only five and kept in the nursery all day. They wouldn't have quarreled *there!*"

"She was furious enough to bring it up for years afterwards, whenever they had a row."

"1953's a long time ago," said Roddy. "Will she still go?"

"I don't see why not," said Andy. "It will have been Andy Coaches' dad who laid her up, and he'll have done it as fussily and tidily as if he was burying an uncle. You remember — no, Roddy won't — what he used to be like about our oiling our bikes at the end of holidays. We'll have to check quite a few things, strip the pumps down and probably renew the washers and so on. And she runs off the accumulator cells from our standby plant — Cousin

Emma, we have our own generator in case of emergencies because the electricity comes to us by an eighteen-mile cable over the hills. I'm pretty certain Father bought a complete new set of cells for the Coronation jaunt, though Anna won't need nearly as many as the house does to get up to power-line voltage — about two dozen, I should think."

"Isn't 1953 a long time ago for a battery?" said Finn. "Car batteries only last a couple of years."

"These are quite different," said Andy. "A car battery is made of six cells joined together, little ones. These are individual cells, two volts each, made to last. They'll take over a thousand cycles of charge and discharge. They may be near the end of their tether, but even so they'll do us, with luck."

"Couldn't we buy new ones?" said Roddy. "I mean, if it's only two dozen."

"Five quid each," said Andy. "A hundred and twenty pounds. I don't mind wasting a bit of my fiber glass, but anything over fifty quid and the party's off."

"Father must have spent more than that on *his* new batteries," said Roddy.

"He needed them," said Andy. "We didn't get on the power line till the year after. Besides, we weren't paupers then."

"And anyway," said Finn, "Mother would have spent a hundred and twenty quid ten times over in London."

"How lovely," sighed Miss Newcombe.

Andy gave a quick frown at Finn and shoved his chair back with a clatter.

"Everybody finished?" he said. "Let's go and have a look at her. Then I'll be able to see how much we've got to do,

28

and whether we can do it with the kit we've got here. High time you got dressed, Poop. These are the decent Highlands, girl."

"I'm sorry," said Miss Newcombe and drifted out, while Emma gazed after her. She had said almost nothing, but the room seemed lifeless without her. The boys were out on the verandah by the time Emma came to from her daze. Finn was laughing quietly as she shifted her dirty plate to the sideboard.

"What's up," said Emma, copying her.

"Andy. Why do you think he's suddenly so keen on faking a monster? *He* knows there's not going to be anything like enough money in it to save the company."

"Oh, yes, I see," said Emma. "He was being squelching, and then he changed his mind. He said it was because he wanted to get the submarine going."

"Well, that's part of it. But the other part is that it might be a way of luring Gabriella up here."

"The girl Roddy was out of date about?"

"That's what Andy *says* . . . he leads a complicated life."

"He looks as if he'd always got everything he wanted," said Emma.

"He has, almost. That's why he was so angry when Gabriella left him flat. He wants his revenge — not on her, I mean — on the people she works with. I'll explain it all to you sometime."

"But what about *you?*" said Emma. "Do you want to go to all this trouble to hoax the TV people? It's only an *idea*. I mean — it probably won't bring you any tourists at all."

"Oh, it's something to pass the time. It might stop the boys from fighting, too. The holidays are always hell, with

Roddy needling Andy and Andy bashing Roddy. Anything for peace."

"There was a sort of row just brewing up, wasn't there?" said Emma. "Was that why you egged me on?"

Finn smiled her calm, secretive smile and jumped the five steps from the verandah in one leap. Emma went down more sedately, a little ashamed at her own unwillingness to risk twisting her ankle on the first day of the holidays. The McAndrews, she felt, were the kind who would risk anything for a spur-of-the-moment whim, even Finn, who seemed so cool. Perhaps they would soon get bored of having their unadventurous cousin to stay.

The boys were already far down the road, Roddy running at a pounding sprint by the water's edge and Andy loping beside him; then the road and shore curved and the corner of the bungalow hid them. By the time the girls reached the corner they had disappeared, presumably into one of the four long, tarred buildings which stood beside a little crooked jetty whose crisscross supports were mirrored in the motionless loch. Emma stopped on the little bridge over the stream and looked about her in surprise; everything before this had seemed so wild, with the road running between the steep hills and the water and then the bungalow itself, which for all its luxury looked like a temporary building, a lodge in the wilderness. But now, where the stream had washed down from the hills a wide arena of soil, she saw stone buildings — stables and barns and a little row of cottages with ornamental carvings above doors and windows. There was even a squat octagonal tower that could only be a dovecote. The line of the buildings carried her eye away from the loch towards the foot of the hill.

"Oh!" she said. "What's that?"

Set at a right angle to the line, close under the hill and looking out over the arena and the loch, stood a house. It was huge and it was blind; not a window along the wide front reflected the day.

"That's Big House," said Finn. "What we live in now is called The Huts. Grandfather built The Huts as a laboratory, and moved down there after the fire. He was going to rebuild Big House, but he never got round to it."

"How long ago?"

"1887. Andy says Grandfather spent the insurance money on setting up the company, but that's nonsense. He was a rich man already, because *his* father had made a lot of money out of building railways. He didn't build them himself, of course — he invested money in them; it was a frightful gamble, but he was lucky and he built Big House to celebrate. Come and look at Anna."

After the sparkling light of the morning the inside of the smallest boathouse seemed dark as a cellar. Dimly in the light from the door Emma could see what looked like a railway freight car — the result, perhaps, of one of her great-great-grandfather's successful gambles. Then she saw that the wheels were too small and too close together, and that the bulk above them was the wrong shape for any sort of tank, pointed at the end and jutting out so far that it would be bound to bash into the next car in the train. She heard Andy's voice in the darkness, and a scraping noise. Then a slit of dazzling light opened at the far end of the shed and widened, as Andy, wading in water up to his knees, heaved a big door open. The boathouse faced east, so that the sunlight bounced blindingly off the water and made silver ripple patterns flow along the underside of *Anadyomene*'s dull hulk.

Yes, there were rails, but they ran at a steep angle straight down into the loch; the wheels were part of a sturdy cradle on which the submarine lay. *Anadyomene* was a dull greenish color, but not the green of paint — rather the green of old cannons outside museums. She was a bit longer than two beds placed end to end — say fifteen feet — and *fat*. Emma had expected something cigar-shaped, like a U-boat, but this was a pointed blob. A man could almost have stood upright in the middle of her, if he got his head into the much smaller blob on top. This second blob, shaped like a squashed bowler hat, must be the conning tower; there was no deck on it — the hull immediately began its curve down to the points at either end and a mirror curve ran up to the points from below. At Andy's end, the point nearest the water, there were four rigid fins and a ridiculous little propeller that looked as if it would hardly have driven a toy boat. When Emma walked up to the top of the shed and looked along the hull she saw that it was exactly circular, with the conning tower squatting on top; she also saw that in the front of the conning tower there was a narrow strip of thick green glass, shaped like the visor slit in a knight's helmet. So this was a submarine you could see out of, supposing you could see anything underwater. Towards the back of the hull, like the flippers of a turtle, two large flat plates jutted out. Andy was meditatively waggling one of them slightly up and down when Roddy fetched a rough wooden ladder from two hooks on the wall, bonked it boomingly against the hull, and scampered up.

"Hold it," said Andy as Roddy started to fiddle with the heavy catch of the lid on top of the conning tower.

"Who says?" said Roddy, and lifted the lid.

At once Andy dashed up the ladder, caught him by the belt of his jeans, and pulled him towards the propeller. Roddy, straddling the hull, clung to the rim of the conning tower until Andy began to tickle him. As soon as he let go Andy started to shove him along the curve of the hull, which grew steeper and steeper, though there was never any danger of his falling. But though he could easily have jumped down he tried uselessly to cling to the gripless metal, shouting, "Stop it! Oh, stop it!" until Finn picked up the ladder and took it along to the stern. When Roddy's foot reached it she seized his heel and placed it on a rung.

"Other leg," she said. "Come on, Roddy. Other leg. You won't fall."

Shiveringly, Roddy swung his other leg over and Finn felt it onto the rung for him; he worked himself by inches onto the ladder and came slowly down; none of the time had he been more than six feet above the ground. Andy stood on the hull above them, hands on hips, grinning like a handsome buccaneer who had just fed his favorite enemy to the sharks.

"He never learns," said Finn to Emma. "He can go up but he can't come down. He's got stuck in more trees than any boy in Scotland."

Roddy seemed to regain all his usual aggression the moment he touched the ground, but at the same time he lost his temper.

"You wait!" he shouted at Andy. "You wait! I'll do — I'll do *something*."

He rushed out of the boathouse.

"What was that about?" said Andy, pretending to be astonished.

"Showing up his weakness in front of Cousin Emma," said Finn. "Andy, you're an oaf."

"She'd better know in case she goes climbing with him," said Andy.

"All right," said Finn. "Cousin Emma, next time Roddy does something you *might* admire, try and say so. Don't cheat — he'll see through that. Can we see inside Anna?"

"No point," said Andy. "I forgot to bring a torch — that's why I didn't want Roddy smashing around in the dark. I'll go up and inspect the generator batteries. The trouble is you can never tell if a cell's just on the verge of going, but I'll be able to check whether any have actually gone. You might think about monster heads; we don't want anything dragonish — there's a book of dinosaurs in the billiard room, or there used to be — you might find something to start you off in that. It mustn't look as if it came off a shield or out of a fairy story. Got it?"

Emma stood in the sunlight and wondered where to start looking for Roddy. From another of the boathouses she heard a banging and scraping and went to investigate. Roddy was dragging a dinghy down the slipway, his face still purple with fury and effort, though every heave only shifted the boat an inch or two over the concrete.

"Can I help?" said Emma. "Are you going for a row?"

"Sail," panted Roddy. "Take off your shoes and socks and catch hold of the thwart there."

Between them they moved it a foot at a time, until they were paddling in the chilly shallows. Suddenly the boat was

34

resting on water rather than the grinding concrete and at the next heave slid with such a rush across the glossy surface that Emma sat down in it and rose soaked to the armpits, to see Roddy hooting with pleasure.

"Run back to The Huts and change," he said. "Give your wet things to Mary. I'll pick you up there. Have you done any sailing?"

"No."

"Good. I'll teach you."

Clammy and clinging though her jeans were, Emma stopped on the verandah to look at Miss Newcombe, who was sunbathing. She lay on her face on an air mattress while a radio disc jockey gibble-gabbled softly at her ear. She was tanned, but not to the solid beechwood brown of the South African heroes and heroines Emma knew; the weaker sun of Scotland had turned her a silky gold all over.

"Dipped in honey," said Emma.

"Yum yum," said Finn, coming out of the main door with a big green book under her arm. "What's happened to you?"

"I fell in the water getting the boat out. Roddy's going to teach me to sail."

"Can you swim?"

"A bit."

"I thought all South Africans . . ."

"I had a sort of eczema, so I wasn't allowed in the sea. But I've been learning at school."

"Then . . . OK, I'll come and draw monsters in the bow. Roddy's a pretty good sailor, but you can get sudden gusts off Ben Goig without a second's warning. Anybody can capsize on *our* loch."

She sounded proud about it. Emma went in and changed,

35

and found a pink-faced girl in the kitchen plucking a chicken. She said she was called Caitlin and showed Emma where to hang her wet clothes. By the time Emma came out, Roddy had his dinghy close up by the road, its tall triangle of sail as yellow as a buttercup and flopping to and fro in the light breeze; he seemed to be arguing with Finn — you could tell from his posture — but they'd settled it by the time Emma was down the steps. Finn tucked herself and her book and her sketching pad into the awkward nook in front of the mast, and Emma climbed in at the stern.

"What was dipped in honey?" said Finn, as though she were changing a conversation which Emma hadn't heard.

"Miss Newcombe," said Emma. "She looked like that."

"Except for being sticky," said Roddy. "Can't you call her Poop, for heaven's sake?"

He obviously had his sulks back.

"I can if she asks me," said Emma. "Are you sure calling her that doesn't make her . . . sort of stay like she is?"

"Her real name's Peony," said Roddy. "You can't expect us to call her *that!*"

"That," echoed the far cliff, faint on the faint breeze.

"She was called Poop when we got her," said Finn.

"She's not a dog!" shouted Roddy, and again the cliff agreed with him.

"What a super echo," said Emma.

"It just works down this one line," said Finn. "That's why Grandfather built The Huts there, so that he could do experiments with sound."

"Father calls her Poop," said Roddy. "He wouldn't if he thought it was bad for her."

"What's your father like?" said Emma. "What does he do? Why isn't he here?"

36

"He's a spy," said Roddy. "Only they never seem to put him up against a wall and shoot him. That would learn him."

"They give you a last wish when they do that," said Finn. "I wonder what his would be."

"To see a falcon stoop," said Roddy.

"To say something witty to a duchess," said Finn.

"To climb Ben Goig," said Roddy.

"Does that help, Cousin Emma?" said Finn.

"What's he doing now?" said Emma.

"Spying," said Roddy. "Against the Swiss."

"Shut up," said Finn. "Father is short and thin and old, but not old-feeling, except on a few bad days. He was very wild when he was young, so he didn't marry until he was fifty-five. He was the only son after a lot of daughters, too, which is why we're a whole generation further up the family tree than you are. He's never had a job, except during wars. I think he may have been a sort of spy once, but now all he's interested in is insects. He knows a lot about locusts, and he's made himself the world's top expert on a sort of beetle that damages cocoa trees in Africa. He's at a conference in Geneva now, all about controlling insect pests with other insects which eat the pests. But although he's never *done* anything, he's been everywhere and seen everything and met everyone. If he finds you reading a Bulldog Drummond book he'll tell how he and Sapper got thrown out of a Marseilles nightclub one evening; and whenever an Honors List is published he has to spend several days writing to all his cronies who've become lords and things. He loves lords. He's very clever and very tough. He ought to have been a great man, but somehow he went along a different road."

"Father's a spy," said Roddy. "He always was and he always will be. When he dies, Saint Peter will meet him at the gate and say, 'Ah, Major McAndrew — we've been waiting for you. We just want you to nip down to the other place and find out one or two things for us.' "

Finn and Emma laughed, and then Roddy started his sailing lesson. He was a rotten teacher, as he tried to explain how a sailing boat can go forward even when the wind seems to be pushing it sideways, or worse. He made it very confusing, and he knew it, and that made him shout. But it was interesting for Emma to notice how suddenly the echo of his shouts died when the boat went out of the line along which the cliff funneled any noise that came to it.

"Show her," said Finn at last. "Shove the tiller about and let her see what happens. She'll work out why — she's that sort."

After that the morning became comfortable again, and soon Emma was holding the tiller while Roddy played around with the set of the sail. Finn passed aft a sketch of a most plausible monster, thin-necked and tiny-headed, before settling down to read her book. The day drowsed towards noon.

"I say," said Finn suddenly. "Here's a bit of luck. Nobody knows why the dinosaurs died out. They all suddenly became extinct at about the same time, and this man thinks it was because the climate got colder. But our loch's warm, which would explain why the creature managed to stick it out here."

"It didn't feel warm when I sat down in it," said Emma.

"It would have felt a good sight colder if it hadn't got

38

warm springs in it," said Roddy. "You could work the fish in too, Finn."

"What about the fish?" said Finn.

"There being no big ones."

"I haven't seen any fish," said Emma, peering down into the extraordinarily clear water.

"They're all up the east end," said Roddy, pointing down the loch. "It's shallow there, and full of plankton and weed and so on, and shoals of little fish, but no big ones because the monster eats them. This is the deep end."

"How deep?" said Emma.

"Nobody knows. It just goes down and down. It's a great crack, with underwater cliffs on each side."

"*My* creature is gentle and herbivorous," said Finn. "He lives on a special sort of weed which only grows in our loch."

"How many are there?" said Emma. "Or does it live for ever?"

"About six at a time."

"Wouldn't it become very inbred?"

"That's all right," said Roddy. "The McAndrews are very inbred too."

"No we're not," said Finn. "The clan married each other for about three generations between the evictions and the railways, but not enough to make us different from other people. My creature *is* very inbred. It lives for about . . . about two hundred years, and the other dinosaurs died out . . . hang on —" she rattled through the leaves of her book and ran her finger down a chart "— sixty million years ago. How many generations is that, Cousin Quick-with-sums?"

"Thirty thousand. No, three hundred thousand."

"Too many," said Roddy. "It'll have to live longer."

"Or have more of them," said Emma.

"There'd have to be more of them anyway," said Roddy. "Otherwise in all that time you'd be bound to have a point when all six were females."

"Eggs," said Finn. "They could lay eggs which stay dormant for ages, couldn't they? We ought to have one to show. They might bury them in the sand like turtles."

"No," said Roddy. "If you practically never see them, they must be like fish and live deep."

"I've given mine nostrils," said Finn. "All the dinosaurs were air-breathers. I think."

"If they laid their eggs *near* the warm springs," said Emma, "and then — Oh!"

A huge white egg popped out of the water beside the boat, patterned with strange ridges. Emma stared, horrified, but only for an instant before the egg spun round and became Miss Newcombe's bathing cap.

"Boo!" she said. She must have swum quite a long way underwater but was hardly panting at all. "Lunchtime, Roddy. Please tow me home. Andy says that something . . . whatever he was doing . . . is all right."

"Did he say anything else?" said Roddy.

"I don't think so."

Roddy threw her a rope and steered home, frowning. Emma watched Miss Newcombe lazily trailing through the water, like a fish that enjoyed being caught; she rehearsed a few admiring words for Roddy's sailing, but it was wasted thought because he bungled the landing, thudding the boat into the beams of the jetty. All she could say was

"Thank you for teaching me to sail," but Roddy only scowled worse. He and Andy needled each other all through lunch while Finn read her dinosaur book and Emma told Miss Newcombe about Botswana.

3

"*I am beginning to understand about the Scots,*" *wrote Emma. "And why they murdered each other so much." She looked out at the loch and wondered whether it was fair to put a thing like a personal quarrel into her diary. Today it was easy to believe in the hot springs, because a band of mist, or steam, lay a few feet above the gently lurching surface. She could see below the band for quite a long way across the water; and above it the skyline, nocked with Darwin's Pimple, stood clear; but the far shore and the echoing cliffs were blanked out.*

Emma decided that the feud between Andy and Roddy was tiresome but interesting, so she'd put it in; when she'd finished the diary she could

*always change her mind and rewrite the pages
where it came. That was an advantage in a loose-
leaf diary. Or perhaps the feud would simply
clear up now that the rain had gone; when they'd
all been cramped together in the hull of* Anadyomene, *the air had been heavy with bad
temper, crackling like the air on the veldt before a thunderstorm.*

*"It might be something to do with the narrow
valleys they live in," she wrote. "The mountains
press in on them, so that they have to break out
or fight each other. It was like that yesterday in
the submarine."*

Emma was sitting in the triangular cavern of metal, with
her back against the motor, carefully rubbing away the
verdigris from the rod of the port after pump, which Andy
had dismantled for her. The emery paper bit into the
green stains until suddenly there were parallel scratches of
yellow; as soon as she saw them she took a sheet of finer
paper and rubbed with that, holding the metal up every
now and then to the light of the bulb that dangled by the
hatch. She thought the pumps were oddly beautiful. There
was something immensely satisfying about the way their
working parts fitted together, so finely made that you could
feel the slight suck of metal as you slid a cleaned shaft along
the groove it was meant for. And the outsides were deco-
rated with a pattern of vine leaves and a panel saying
ROPER'S INVINCIBLE EXTRACTOR. FIFTEEN GOLD MEDALS.
There was a picture of the gold medals under the words;
you could see the bearded head of Napoleon III on the top
one, but the artist had had to overlap the others to get them

43

all in so that only the backs of the royal heads showed, with sometimes a royal ear.

Roddy craned over the motor to see what she was doing.

"They aren't kings at all," he said. "They're all impostors. That one was a sheep rustler, and that one was a forger."

"Napoleon the Third was a real impostor, sort of," said Finn.

"A real impostor and not a fake one," said Roddy in an explaining voice. "A fake impostor isn't an impostor at all. He is what he's pretending to be, and he's only pretending he isn't."

"Shut up," said Finn. "Napoleon was a waiter before he was an emperor. He used to boast that he could carve ham thinner than any monarch in Europe, but then he started the Franco-Prussian War and lost it, and his friends weren't interested in the ham any more. That's all true. Father told me."

"When was the war?" said Roddy.

"Eighteen seventy-something. Nearly twenty years before Grandfather thought of Anna."

"He didn't think of her," said Roddy. "He pinched the idea from a Frenchman. What was his name?"

"Goubet," said Andy's voice above their heads. Emma sensed Roddy going tense and looked up. Andy's face was upside-down, poking through the hatch.

"Get it right," he said sarcastically. "Monsieur Goubet built two submarines, but they weren't much good because they wouldn't stay level in the water. He cast the hull of the first one out of a single bit of bronze, so that he didn't have any leaky seams, and he had the notion of using an

44

electric motor. Grandfather got him to cast a second hull, for Anna, and he pinched the idea of the motor. But he invented a quite different control system, like modern submarines. He was a clever old cove. Anna *works*."

The head, crimson with the effort of its upside-down lecture, whisked out of sight again. Roddy was beginning to relax when a pair of gum boots dangled from the hatch, followed by bare knees, a brown kilt, a naked wet torso, and Andy's head the right way up.

"I've had a notion," said Andy. "Those old batteries *are* OK, but they might go any moment. It would be far safer to have new ones, and it struck me that what we're doing is really publicity for the company. We could buy some new ones and swing it on the company accounts. It would be allowable against tax, and we'd finish up with twenty-four fresh batteries for the generator."

"How much?" said Roddy.

"I rang up Fort William. It comes to just over a hundred and thirty quid."

"You can't do it!" shouted Roddy, trying to leap up and banging his head on the bronze hull. "You can't do it!" he said again as he floundered. "It's the shareholders' money. You've no right to waste the shareholders' money furthering your own amours. I bet there's something in the Companies Acts about it. I'll write to Old Crow and ask him."

"Vote, Finn," said Andy nonchalantly.

"No thanks," said Finn. "It sounds quite a good idea about the tax, if it would work, but you know Old Crow would be against a wangle like that if it came to a vote; and it isn't right to outvote him on this kind of thing — he'd be terribly hurt."

45

"OK," said Andy, very dignified. "I'll go and get the best of the old ones. We'll probably get stuck without any juice, thanks to your pigheadedness, and . . ."

"If it's going to be dangerous . . ." Emma began.

Andy laughed, dashing and scornful.

"Canny girl. But it shouldn't be too bad. The pumps are hand operated, so we should be able to float up. In fact I think you probably drive the thing in a slightly buoyant state and use the hydroplanes to force her under, so that if she stops she'll automatically bob up. Roddy may make us the laughingstock of Scotland, but he isn't going to drown us."

Andy lifted his arms to the rim of the hatch and flicked himself out, supple as a gymnast.

The others chattered on, relaxed and easy. Emma was glad to know that it was possible to ease Roddy's temper with banter, as well as by sitting down in cold water. She didn't want to have to do that every half hour. Then Andy's boots dangled through the hatch again and the rage-storm inside the bronze cave brewed up until Emma's skin prickled. Andy had brought a steel tape to measure a few dimensions, but did not explain why and left in silence. It had been very close quarters for three people, as *Anadyomene* was only built for two. The crew were supposed to sit back to back in the exact center of the boat, with their heads poking up into the conning tower so that one could look out through the glass slit forward, and the other through a similar slit towards the stern. They were going to have a lot to do, Emma thought, each with one pair of pumps to handle, while the man who faced forward steered and the man who faced aft was in charge of the engine and the flipperlike hydroplanes. All those levers! But if Andy

46

was right about how you made Anna go, it meant you worked the pumps until she was almost sinking, letting water flood into the four ballast tanks below. After that you left them alone and could concentrate on the other things. It might be possible with practice, but Emma was very glad it wouldn't be her problem. Even on dry land the submarine's hull felt like a prison, a trap; she hated to imagine what it would be like to mutter along below the surface, with the chill water above and below pressing in against every square inch of its surface, seeping through by the propeller shaft and the hydroplane pivots, and waiting — if you got deep, too deep — to crush the bronze bubble as you crumple a sweet paper in your fist before throwing it away.

Emma was getting on well with her pump when there came a clumping on the hull above them and she sensed Roddy going tense again. Andy's boots came through the hatch until they were standing on the steering seat; then she heard a scraping on the hull; his bare midriff tensed with an effort taking place out of sight, and the head and shoulders slid through the hatch with a rush; last of all came the arms, lowering a wooden crate. It was obviously heavy. Andy would have found the job easier if Roddy had been on the hull above him to lower it down. But Andy wouldn't ask and Roddy wouldn't offer, so Andy was putting the pressure on by showing that he could do the job himself. He slid the crate along towards where Emma was working.

In it she saw three black slabs, each as big as a family Bible but with a filler cap and two terminals on the top.

"I'll have to build a frame for these," he said as he picked them out of the crate. "We don't want them sliding about. In fact, I'll have to build four frames, if we're going to trim the boat properly."

"Couldn't you do it with car batteries?" said Finn. "You'd only need four of them in all. One out of your Lotus, one out of my ol' banger, one out of Poop's car and one off one of the tractors."

"It would work," said Andy, "but it'd only give us forty minutes running time, at the most. These jobs would give four hours when they were new, so they should still be good for at least two."

As soon as he was out of the hatch Emma tried to pick one of the cells up and found it too heavy to manage at the angle she was kneeling. He came back almost at once with three more, but when he had twelve of the cells stacked neatly on either side of the rear seat he disappeared for quite a long time. Emma finished her pump and edged around the cells towards the hatch, steadying herself by holding onto a little wheel which obviously turned a shaft running down into the center of the keel. In fact there was an arrow showing which way to turn it, and the words "Weight Release" embossed on its upper surface. "Weight" reminded her about the batteries. She was frowning as she climbed out.

Andy was standing in the doorway of the boathouse, naked to the waist still, but calmly smoking one of his little cheroots and watching the drumming rain as though his hair were not sending little chilling rivulets all down his brown back. There was a wheelbarrow beside him, covered with a piece of plastic sheeting.

"I've finished my pump," said Emma.

"Great," he said, turning round. "I'll fit it together in a tick."

"Why don't you wear a mackintosh?"

"We've a feud with the Macintoshes. They stole some of our sheep in 1423."

"No, but seriously."

"Seriously, Cousin Emma, I'd sweat like a pig if I had to lug these cells around in any sort of waterproof. I'll tell you a secret about rain which all good Scotsmen know — it gets you only as wet as you think it does. If you cringe along with your collar turned up and your shoulders hunched, you get soaked to the skin; but tell yourself that it's only a bit of mist and stride through it, and you'll find you can shake off the few drops that stick to you like a dog does."

"How much do the cells weigh?"

"About ten pounds apiece."

"What happened to the old batteries? The ones that were put in her when she was built?"

"They're still there — you'd have to hack them up to get them out."

"So you're putting a lot of *extra* weight in. Will that be safe? Will she still float?"

"Sure thing. Andy Coaches told me that Father had a hell of a time getting her to go under at all in Coronation Year. He remembers bringing some big stones down to make extra ballast. We may have to do the same — or I thought I might ship a few extra cells, in case some of these go while she's going."

"Oh, *that's* all right. Shall I help you with these? I could lower them down to you."

Emma lifted the plastic sheet aside and saw that the barrow contained an electric fan heater as well as another batch of cells.

49

"What's that for?" she said. "If you can think yourself dry, can't you think yourself warm?"

"I can, but I can't think an electric motor dry. If it were a smaller job I'd unbolt it and put it in Caitlin's oven, but as it is I'll have to do the job with hot air, like a politician. Mary says it's time for lunch, so we'll give it a blast while we're eating. Did your stomach tell you it was one o'clock, or were you looking for me?"

"I suppose I wanted to know about the weight."

"The batteries sinking Anna? Cautious little Saxon, aren't you? Hi, you don't think I'm going to risk *your* life in this contraption?"

"I don't expect you want to risk anybody's."

"Oh, no one would miss the odd McAndrew. Look, the rain's letting up. Nip back now and you won't get wet. I'll bring the others."

Emma raced home, leaping between puddles and wondering whether she had missed a chance to ask Andy to be nicer to Roddy, or whether that would just drive him deeper into the feud. She stood on the verandah and watched a fresh wall of rain come swishing up the loch and blot out the landscape; through it the three McAndrews scuttered, soaked and laughing, up the steps.

The drenching seemed to wash the quarrel away, for the moment at least, and lunch was a cheerful meal. Halfway through his first helping, Andy slapped his knife and fork onto the table and said, "I've got it!" They all looked at him.

"I thought it was fishy," he said. "Cousin Emma making such a fuss about one or two of us drowning in Anna."

"I don't think it's fishy at all," said Finn. "She doesn't want to spend her holidays going to funerals, especially Scots ones. When we want to be mournful we can outmourn any nation on earth."

"Ingenious but wrong," said Andy. "She does want to spend her holidays going to a funeral — a triple one. If only one or two of us drown, there'll be some left over."

"Bags I be remainder," said Roddy.

"Cousin Emma's evil scheme is to do us all three in together," said Andy.

"How?" said Finn. "Will it be comfortable?"

"I don't know the details yet," said Andy, "but I doubt it."

"She's got a tame monster," said Roddy. "A Botswanan one. That's why she was so interested in ours, I bet you. She's brought hers here in a crate labeled 'Fancy Umbrellas,' and she's going to sneak it into the lake to gobble us up. Now she's worried in case Anna and her monster collide, thus giving the plot away. She spent the whole of this morning polishing Napoleon's nose, which is a sure sign of nerves."

"I didn't see a crate," said Finn.

"British Rail have lost it," said Roddy. "It's sitting in a siding at Rugby. It might get out one night and gobble up the Stationmaster. She's worried about that, too."

"But why?" said Emma slowly. "I mean, I hate books where it turns out that the murderer was just mad. It's — it's inartistic. I must have a reason."

"Hear, hear," said Finn. "I don't mind having a mad cousin in the family, but I draw the line at an inartistic one."

"Nobody would notice a mad one," said Roddy.

"Oh heavens," said Andy, "how dim can you get? Haven't you realized that with us out of the way all this would belong to Cousin Emma?"

He waved a forkful of beef at the watery landscape. Roddy picked up his chair and shifted it a few ostentatious inches away from Emma and nearer Miss Newcombe. Emma gulped and felt her scalp prickle: to own a loch, a mountain, a liniment company! And all (apart from the company) so beautiful. She saw the others looking at her, even Miss Newcombe, and knew that in Andy's joke there were cruel little crumbs of something else, like sand in lettuce.

"Emma darling," said Miss Newcombe very seriously. "If anything *did* happen to the children, might I please stay here?"

"It's all right, Poop," said Andy. "I've put a bit in my will about that. Cousin Emma not to inherit unless Poop Newcombe is granted security of tenure, with rights of socage, spillage and ullage."

"But what about *old* Andy?" said Miss Newcombe. "The Major?"

"It's a condition of Father's will too."

"I expect it is," whispered Finn.

"But aren't there lots of other cousins?" said Emma. "You told me my great-grandfather had lots of daughters."

"It's a sad story," said Finn.

"A sad, sad story," said Andy and Roddy in chorus.

"Don't worry, darling," said Miss Newcombe. "When they say that, like that, all together, it's a sort of joke — or at least they think it is. I sometimes wonder, in my bath for instance, what they'd say if they *really* wanted to tell someone a sad story."

"Shut up, Poop," said Finn. "I want to tell Cousin Emma a really sad story. Your grandmother was our grandfather's favorite daughter, and when she married he was inconsolable."

"In-con-solable," said Andy and Roddy together.

"The Huts was full of gabbling girls, with no one to keep them in order, and his only son was miles away at a horrible English prep school. So to keep himself occupied he bought a parrot. He had a theory about the origins of language, and he thought a parrot might —"

"But they don't know what they're saying," said Emma.

"Aha! Grandfather had a new idea. He didn't try to teach the parrot English — he tried to teach himself parrot. He sat on the verandah all day long, squawking at the bird and listening to it squawking back. His diaries are full of notes of noises — I'll show you. Everybody finished? Shall I ring?"

"You haven't told her why it's a sad story," said Roddy crossly.

"You're the worst storyteller this side of Inverness," said Andy.

Mary came in pushing the trolley with a vast bowl of fruit salad on it and started to collect the dirty plates.

"Sorry," said Finn. "The point is, Cousin Emma, that the endless squawking drove half the girls mad and they had to be shut up, and the other half caught psittacosis from the parrot and died."

"Mary," said Emma. "Would you please tell me if any of that's true?"

"It's true about the parrot, and himself sitting there squealing at it, if that's what Miss Finn's been been telling you."

"But is it the reason why none of the girls married except my grandmother?"

"Ach, nonsense. Himself was a bit of an old tyrant and liked to be mollycoddled. He wouldn't have any of his daughters marrying, and by the time he passed away they were all a bit elderly, poor things."

"But my grandmother . . ."

"*Ran* away, *she* did. Weren't they telling you that? Indeed it is more interesting than all their nonsense —"

"Shh, Mary," said Finn. "We've been keeping it from her."

"She'll have to know now," said Roddy.

"You see, Cousin Emma," said Andy, "there was this Russian prince who fell in love with your grandmother when he spied her from afar at a Highland Gathering at Balmoral. Instantly, he insinuated himself into the bosom of the family, disguised as a —"

"Labrador retriever?" said Emma, seizing the moment when Andy was slopping a spoonful of fruit into his mouth. She had noticed all the McAndrews using the pauses of eating as a method of thinking up their next lie without seeming to hesitate.

"Shut up. You have no soul, you beastly Saxon. Romance means nothing to you. He disguised himself as a second under-footman, so great was the sacrifice he was prepared to make for love. He paid secret court to your grandmother, poor foolish girl. Her heart was won. The night was fixed. The carriage was ordered, with muffled wheels. A sloop waited at Mallaig, ready to whisk them

54

back to the splendors of the Imperial Court. With a beating heart she waited at her window. Came the rattle of hooves on the bridge. Head high, she walked into the utter dark and climbed up beside the driver. One kiss, then the whip cracked and they were away."

"How super," sighed Miss Newcombe.

"It wasn't as super as all that, actually. Her clock was fast and she'd climbed up beside a traveling trouser salesman called Tupper, who hadn't been having much luck in the Highlands because of our preference for the kilt. He'd only stopped to ask the way, but after that kiss —"

Andy made the mistake of stopping for another mouthful. Emma, who normally lived in a world of facts, suddenly felt that she could do it too.

"Let me guess the rest," she said. "Everybody in the house rushed wildly in pursuit and was never seen again. The Russian had gone away to prepare for the elopement, and now when he arrived at the right time he found the house empty. So he just waited. He waited for years, and in the end he married and had two boys and a girl. He's still alive, but he has to pretend to be interested in beetles so that he can go away to Geneva when anybody comes who might notice his Russian accent. Why don't you all go back to Moscow and claim the throne of the Czars? I'm going to have a double helping of *my* cream. Will you please tell me the real story some time, Mary?"

"Indeed I will, Miss Emma. But look, it is leaving off raining. Isn't that a miracle?"

"Hurrah," said Miss Newcombe. "I'll be able to sunbathe."

It was true. In ten minutes the rainstorm had picked up its skirts and bustled away to trouble other valleys, and pale sunbeams lit the whole rinsed landscape. Emma thought of the dark, cramped hole inside the submarine and thought at the same moment of a way of separating Roddy and Andy for the afternoon.

"Can I climb up to Darwin's Pimple?" she said. "I'd love to do that, if Roddy could sail me over and show me the way."

"Um," said Andy. "Poop could go too."

"I'll look after the boat while they climb to the top," said Miss Newcombe. "It's quite a good place to sunbathe, if there aren't any horseflies."

"No you won't," said Andy. "You'll climb to the very top. I'll have my telescope out to make sure you get there. You're fat."

Roddy slid away from the table.

"No I'm not. Honestly. I weighed myself yesterday. Or the day before."

"I bet you're at least a pound over the magic number. Father wouldn't like that if he turned up suddenly. Go and weigh yourself."

"But it means taking all my clothes off."

"Poop," said Finn. "If you're right you'd have to take your clothes off to sunbathe. If you're wrong you'll have to take them off to put on thicker ones. So you'll have to take them off anyway."

"Yes . . . I suppose so," said Miss Newcombe, and left the room frowning. As soon as her footsteps had disappeared across the hall Roddy nipped in.

"How much?" said Finn.

"Twelve pounds," said Roddy.

Andy jumped up, all good temper forgotten.

"You miserable little idiot," he said. "She's bound to realize something's wrong. Can't you ever behave sensibly?"

"Oh, I am a ninny," simpered Roddy. "I meant *ounces.*"

It was just as though he wanted to get the feud going again, thought Emma. Andy, having lost his temper, had no way of getting it back. Yesterday he had deliberately demonstrated Roddy's poor head for heights in front of Emma, so now Roddy had got his own back by deliberately making him lose his cool in front of her. He went very white, opened and closed his mouth once or twice, and started round the table. Roddy edged away, and in the nick of time Mary wheeled the big trolley in, parked it between the boys, and started to clear the table. Emma thought Finn had probably rung for her on purpose.

"Sorry, Mary," said Roddy to her as he sat down and started to scoop peach segments into his mouth. He managed to gobble very smugly. Andy thumped to the sideboard, cut himself a piece of cheese, and thumped out eating it.

"But she *isn't* fat," whispered Emma.

"Not yet," said Finn. "But she will be if she doesn't take exercise. She needs a lot. If she were a pig, she'd be what they call a good doer. Father wrote her proper weight on her bathroom wall before he left, but she won't believe a few ounces count, so she lets herself go for a couple of pounds and then she panics because she can't get rid of it in a few days, and then she stops eating anything at all, which makes her ill and miserable. And when she does get back to the magic number she rings up the baker in Mallaig and gets him to send out two dozen cream buns and eats them

57

at a sitting. It's kinder to fiddle her scales; she'll be blissful when she gets back from her walk and finds she's lost all twelve ounces."

Roddy threw back his chair and dashed for the door as though he'd forgotten an appointment.

"I'll bring the boat round," he called.

"Andy's turn now," said Finn. "I wonder what he'll do."

"Can't you stop them?"

"Not my business — I've always been neutral. The trouble is that Roddy knows how to get Andy's goat in little ways, like just now, but Andy can't do it to Roddy so he has to go in for the big stuff. That's why the rows always look like Andy's fault, but it isn't true. It doesn't usually start on the first day of the holidays, like this — I expect it's partly because Andy's love life is in a mess, and because you're here, and Father isn't."

"I *can* go to my uncle," said Emma.

"Oh, rubbish, don't think of it. Father would be furious, and in any case the row will probably blow over as soon as we've got Anna going. Hi, Poop, what luck?"

"I'm a whole pound over," said Miss Newcombe, in an accent of such horror that she might have found a corpse on her bathroom floor. "I shall have to stop eating potatoes . . . and scones . . . and things."

She was wearing slim blue corduroy trousers and a heavy, dark-blue, polo-necked jersey, which made her look like the film star in those films where the heroine falls into the sea and gets lent some manly fisherman's kit by the hero who happens to have rescued her — only Miss Newcombe looked real, in a way that those heroines seldom do.

"It's all right," said Finn in a comforting voice. "A quick

58

walk up to Darwin's Pimple will take it off. It goes as fast as it comes."

"Not *always*," said Miss Newcombe. "Look, there's Roddy."

"What are you going to do, Finn?" said Emma.

"Rub brasses in Anna. But I'm not going to reason with Andy, if that's what you're getting at. And I advise you not to try your wiles on Roddy."

In a mild breeze they digested their way across the loch. Too soon Roddy started to bark a flurry of captainly orders and the echoing cliff barked back; flustered, Emma got the little jib in and lowered the mainsail without making a mistake, although everything seemed to happen slowly and clumsily; just as she straightened up, panting but pleased with herself among the heaps of canvas, the keel slid with a mild grunt into the shingle of a little cove. It was like being shoved unexpectedly in the back; she floundered to keep her balance, but her feet were still tangled in sail while the top half of her was toppling forward; her thigh banged the thwart; her feet came free just as her wrists plunged into three inches of water; she tried to flip herself onto dryness by way of a handstand and almost made it, but after teetering for an instant fell helplessly back. When the splash was over she was kneeling in a foot of wet, her whole front drenched and water slopping around her calves. Sulkily, she crawled ashore and stood up.

Roddy was whooping like a gull, and the joke was also simple enough for Miss Newcombe. The sight of her so golden and happy completely wiped out Emma's crossness, and she laughed too; then she rolled up her jeans so that

59

the wet part was no longer rubbing like sandpaper at her calves and shins, and took off her shoes and socks. Roddy dug in the little locker by the tiller and threw her a pair of rope-soled sandals; she tried them on.

"I'm afraid they're a bit big," she said. "They're all right for slopping about in, but I can't climb a mountain like this."

"Mountain!" shouted Roddy. "You're not climbing a mountain. It's a hummock, a molehill, a blob! *Those* are mountains!"

He flung out a pointing arm, like Columbus' lookout man spying land, and Emma looked across the loch. Now that they were right over on the far side, the steep rise behind Big House no longer formed the skyline. Behind it had risen a pale ridge, bluish but with white smears of snow along the crest, which vanished at its eastern end into the dark, almost plum-blue wall of the storm cloud.

"That one's Ben Goig," he said. "Over three thousand feet. You can't see Loch Goig from here, of course, but its surface is higher than Darwin's Pimple. We're only going up a few hundred feet. Come on."

The cove was right up against the western end of the cliffs, and Roddy took them up a steep path, which twisted back and ran only a foot or two from the drop; he had brought the boat hook from the dinghy and used it to thwack the heather every few steps, to frighten the adders away, he said. When they reached the highest point of the cliff the path turned inland, winding southward up the long, dull slope. All Roddy's impatience frothed up during the climb; he would surge ahead, thwacking and whistling, until he was almost fifty yards in front; then he would lean on his boat hook and jeer at the others while they toiled up to him, Miss Newcombe climbed earnestly, frowning and pink in the face, with little drops of sweat beading her delicate skin. Emma, born and bred in a country where they take snakes very seriously indeed, was slowed not only by that ancient dread but also by Roddy's tiresome sandals, which slithered on the steep places and rubbed her heels at every footstep. In the end she fought the snake fear down and climbed barefooted. It took them less than an hour, even so, to come out onto a gentler slope and arrive triumphant at the cairn. Roddy was reading the brass plaque let into its side, so Emma did the same.

> To the Honored Memory of
> Charles Robert Darwin
> (1809–1882)
> who, first of all men,
> saw what lay
> "In the dark backward and abysm of Time."
> A. J. McA. 1890

Emma shivered at the mysterious words.

"Grandfather took a long time to decide to do the right thing by him, didn't he?" said Roddy. "Eight years after he died."

"It's a funny place," said Miss Newcombe.

"What do you mean?" said Roddy.

"I've often wondered . . . when you're all away . . . I look out and wonder why he didn't put it *on top*. Up there."

She pointed along the mottled ridge, which continued to slope gently up towards the east, not reaching its highest point for several hundred yards.

"He had something to hide," said Roddy in his darkest voice.

"A body, I expect," said Emma. "Somebody who knew I was the rightful heir."

"Bang on, Cousin Emma. It's old Mother Mulligatawny buried inside there with her crystal ball. She peered into it and saw that in sixty years a rightful heir would get herself born, so she came and blackmailed Grandfather, and he did her in."

"Poisoned her with liniment," said Emma.

"And then he hid her by making her grave conspicuous."

"It does smell a bit . . . funny," said Miss Newcombe. As she sniffed the clean upland air tiny puckers appeared on either side of her delicious nose. Roddy laughed and started to rush about the hillside, bashing the bushes and stooping every now and then to pick something up. Emma stayed where she was and looked about her. Ben Goig shut off the north, and the ridge they were standing on ran east into a muddle of higher hills. She walked around the cairn and looked south; this was a broader valley, with no loch in it; instead, most of the bottom was divided into real fields, among which stood several dwellings. A white house with dark-blue window frames and doors nestled into a little wood less than a mile down the slope.

"That's Fertagh," said Roddy, rushing up the slope with an armful of small rocks.

"Does it belong to you — to me, I mean?" said Emma.

Roddy scowled. He dropped his rocks at the foot of the cairn, chose one from the pile, fitted it into a cranny, and banged it tight with another one.

"It ought to, but it doesn't," he said. "Some of the Mc-Andrews fought for Prince Charlie in 1745, and some of us didn't. When it was over King George rewarded the traitors by giving them the best land, and left the honest men the barren bits. They're McAndrews down there, and Father is their Chief, but the land doesn't belong to us. Bother, I was hoping to see the islands. You sometimes can, after rain."

Emma followed his gaze towards the west and at first thought she was looking out over another valley, enormously wide and full of mist, to where a couple of hills rose. Then she saw that the mist was sea.

"Those are islands, aren't they?" she said. "Isn't that one a funny shape?"

"Eigg? Yes, it used to be a volcano, and so was Skye, over there, and Ardnamurchan, which you can't see down in the south. But on a good day you can see the outer islands, the Hebrides, sixty miles away. Sometimes when the sun is going down and all the sky is marmalade-colored you notice that the edge of the sea has a lump on it, and that's South Uist. It looks holy — the sort of island in the west you are supposed to go to when you're dying, and then your soul goes straight to heaven. What's the matter, Poop?"

"I was just wondering. If Mother . . . I've forgotten her name . . . died *all* that time ago you wouldn't expect her to be still . . ."

She wrinkled her nose again and sniffed the impeccable air.

"I rather think it's another sad story," said Emma.

"That's right," said Roddy. "A sad, sad story."

"Oh good," said Miss Newcombe. But she still looked puzzled.

4

"Yesterday was terrifying," wrote Emma. She looked out at the loch and thought about its lightless depths, where the underwater cliffs went down and down. It was a day like the first day, with the water still as glass and no belt of steam above it. Noticing that set her wondering about the hot springs, and Finn's ingenious idea that the warmth allowed the monster to survive the Ice Ages. But if they'd been hot enough for that, wouldn't the monster have boiled? She had an idea that the ice cap had been hundreds of feet thick up here in Scotland. She wondered whether there was a book in the billiard room in which she could check. She was surprised at her own determination to make the monster a possible

idea, to find out facts which would prove that it could have happened. Partly this was because she felt that she couldn't often match the wild inventions of the McAndrews, but she could at least be thorough, and impress them that way; but partly it was because she had caught some of her own father's obsession with the survival of wildlife — in a mad way it would be making up for the trophies in the dining room and the awful, beautiful tiger skins in the hall if she could somehow use her wits to make this other, imagined creature as real as possible. The mere idea of an animal coming through for sixty million years was comforting, even if it wasn't true.

"Yesterday was terrifying." She nearly crossed the words out again, but left them. "We had some quite useful ideas at breakfast," she wrote.

"We must have a broken net to show them, as well as a film," said Finn. "And a couple of fishermen with a story of how they were bringing their net in and there was this great thing threshing around which almost capsized their boat before it broke the net."

"Good," said Andy. "Ewan Uphill can do it with Andy Coaches — they can be father and son."

"Andy Ghillie's more photogenic than Andy Coaches," said Finn. "He's gnarleder."

"He's nothing like so good a liar," said Roddy.

"He lies beautifully in the Gaelic," said Finn. "It's just talking English makes him sound so shifty, because he's not used to it. Ewan can translate — they'll love that."

"Where are you going to get your net?" said Roddy ag-

65

gressively. "And how are you going to stop them realizing there are no fish in the loch big enough to net?"

"City nits won't know that," said Andy. "I'll shop around for an old net next time I'm in Mallaig — someone's always got a torn one that's not worth mending."

"I had an idea," said Emma cautiously. They looked at her.

"It's about why no one has heard of the monster before. If you said that it only appears once every twenty-seven years, that means last time was 1944 and the time before was 1917, which were both war years and anyone who might have made a fuss was away fighting."

"*Very* good," said Andy. "And it helps with something that's been bothering me. I know telly folk, and they don't send camera teams dashing about for fun. They're far more likely to send a scout up first, and that would mean two lots of faking. But if it only pops up for a few days, at long intervals, they'd have to come up quickly or they'd miss it. We might even be able to tell them where to look for it without giving the show away."

"It seems a crazy way for a monster to carry on," said Roddy.

"Mating season," said Finn. "Not every year, every twenty-seven."

"Only one of it?" said Roddy. "Some love life!"

His wicked glance flashed across at Andy, who luckily missed the look and the meaning.

"It could be a single bull which had beaten the other males in the herd," said Emma.

"Fearsome deep-water battles," said Finn with relish.

"And then it swims in a regular pattern across the loch, a

bit further each day," said Emma. "It could be fertilizing the eggs, or something."

"If we know too much about why it does what it's doing that'll look fishy," said Finn.

"Right," said Andy in his officer voice. "This is the way we'll play it. We'll think up as watertight a story as we can, including why it does what it does, but we won't tell the telly folk any of the reasons. With a bit of luck they'll work it out for themselves, and that'll make them feel so smug that they won't even consider the possibility that we've worked it all out before them."

"Besides," said Finn, "it's better to have a bit of a mystery. Then they can put on that mysterious voice."

"And still," said Roddy, plummily, "the murky depths of the loch retain their terrifying secret. What further evidence will come to light, to reveal to the world the true nature of the Curse of the McAndrews? Only time can tell."

"That's it," said Finn.

"When are we going to take Anna out?" said Roddy.

"I've had the batteries on charge all night," said Andy. "It'll take Ewan and me about an hour to shift them in to Anna and connect up. Then we'll tow her round to the jetty with the tractor and Finn and I will take her out. We'll only go far enough to see if she's watertight, and then we'll come in again."

"You could do that outside her own shed, without all that towing," said Roddy.

"No I couldn't. If I take her out down the big slipway, Ewan can sit at the top with the tree-felling cable run out to the shackle in Anna's nose. Then if anything goes wrong he can simply haul us out."

"I'll run the tractor," said Roddy. "You needn't waste Ewan's time."

"Not on your life," said Andy. "Not on *my* life, I mean. I'm not having you larking about on the other end of the towrope while Finn and I are underwater."

"Have you thought," said Roddy, "that when your telly folk are here they'll smell a rat if you aren't somewhere about too? And Finn? Who's going to run Anna *then*, Mr. Big?"

"I'm taking her out this morning," said Andy sharply. "See you at the boathouse in about an hour, Finn."

He pushed his chair back and stalked out, as though that settled everything. Roddy opened a Coke bottle with a wrench and hurled the cap out through the open window; its small splash spoiled the still surface of the water, but only for an instant.

Before the hour was up Roddy's impatience was too much for his dignity. He fussed in and out of Emma's room until she had to stop writing to her parents and go with him down to the boathouse to see what was happening. They found a big blue tractor chugging to itself outside the door and as they approached, a young man came out of the boathouse and switched it off. He was tall, red-faced and fair-haired.

"Ewan," said Roddy, "this is our cousin Emma Tupper. Emma, this is Ewan McAndrew, Ewan Uphill, we call him. Emma's the granddaughter of the aunt who ran away."

"Yess," said Ewan. "Mary was telling us. It must be grand to come home, Miss Emma."

He spoke very softly and shyly, but with no accent

Emma could hear apart from a slight lingering hiss where a word ended with an "s."

"It's lovely," said Emma.

"How much cable have you got on here?" said Roddy, fiddling with the levers of the large winch which the tractor carried behind it, like a Victorian lady's bustle.

"Hundred and fifty yards," said Ewan. "Hark to that, now."

A whining hum rose from the boathouse. Roddy dashed in, and Emma followed in time to hear the whine beginning to fail as the little propeller of the submarine slowed from a blur to its own shape, and stopped. Andy's head poked out of the hatch.

"Not bad," he said. "Poop, what on earth do you think you're doing?"

Emma turned and saw Finn and Miss Newcombe in the doorway, Miss Newcombe wearing her ivory-colored dressing gown and looking as though she were just going sleepy to bed. Ewan's red face turned a shade redder, but it was hard to tell whether this was pleasure or embarrassment.

"Oh, it's all right," said Miss Newcombe. "I mean, Mary says you're going to drown yourselves, so I thought I'd better be ready to rescue you. It's just that this is warmer for waiting around in than my bathing wrap. There's always such a lot of waiting around — like films."

"Mary's always said we were going to drown," said Andy, as he climbed out. "Ever since I can remember, the moment any of us even paddled in the loch . . ."

"It's that great-aunt of hers who was gifted with the gifts," said Finn. "Mary feels she's got to keep the family reputation up by prophesying the odd bit of doom."

69

"Shut up," said Andy. "Come and look at this."

He led them to the very back of the shed, where an ugly, greasy arrangement of large iron cogs was connected to a big drum with steel cable wound many times around it. Andy picked up four bars of wood and slotted them into grooves at the edge of the outermost cog, so that they became four spokes by which the cog could be turned. The whole thing, Emma saw, was a winch like the one on the tractor, but . . .

"Isn't there an *engine?*" said Emma. "We can't lift that!"

She gestured at the green hulk of *Anadyomene*.

"Yes you can," said Andy. "Finn and I shifted her up an inch or two yesterday, just to see. It's all done by gearing. Look."

He leaned his weight against one of the spokes and turned it through the full circle. Emma heard the wheels groan on the rails and saw the cable tauten and creep a quarter of an inch towards the winch. Still holding the spoke in position with one hand, Andy flipped an iron lug over so that it slotted between the teeth of the outermost cog.

"That locks it," he said. "Now the weight's on the cable and you can knock the chocks off the rails. There's a big split pin through them, Roddy, which you'll have to punch out. I put some penetrating oil on them last night, so they should come easy enough; hammer and punch bar on that beam there — put the pins and chocks up there when you've got them out. I'm going with Ewan to decide the best place for the tractor, and if I'm not back you can start letting her down to the water. OK?"

Roddy yawned. "I think we *might* be able to manage,"

he said in servile tones. "But if it's very difficult we'll come and fetch you, shall we?"

"Do that," said Andy, and stamped out.

"Can't you let him alone for a day or two?" said Finn. "It's not much fun for Cousin Emma."

"You ask *him!*" shouted Roddy. *"He* started it!"

He snatched the hammer and a short iron bar and dived under the trolley, where he began to bang so furiously at the rails that the whole shed rang with the clanking.

"Of course," said Finn, "Andy can be pretty irritating when he puts on that quarterdeck voice. You'll just have to stick it out, and let's hope we can lure Gabriella up with the telly folk — that should ease things a bit."

"I'm glad I'm not one of the clans the McAndrews had feuds with," said Emma.

"Oh, we weren't as rough as some of the others. We're a very little clan, for one thing — not a vulgar great hotch-potch like the Macdonalds. And there's a canny streak somewhere which has kept us out of real trouble. There were always a few McAndrews on the winning side in any war; and we were sensible about who we picked a fight with. Father swore a feud ten years ago, against a firm which was trying to export kippers to California and stole our tartan to wrap them in; he got these kippers flown out to him whenever he went abroad and sent them back sea mail to the managing director, from places like Aden and Honolulu, so that they plopped stinking onto the man's doormat. It wasn't much of a feud, not like the one Grand-father had with Prince Albert over a McAndrew who went as a footman to Balmoral and —"

"Right!" yelled Roddy, hurtling from under the trolley. He slammed his tools and some bits of metal back on the

71

beam, ran to the winch, and threw his weight against a spoke. Nothing happened. He clawed at the lug which locked the outer cog, but that too was immovable. He was such a picture of wrath, crimson-cheeked and panting between clenched teeth, that it was hard not to laugh at him. Finn calmly hauled at a spoke and took the weight off the lug so that Roddy could lift it out from between the cog teeth.

"Right!" he snarled. "Let's have her in the water before Mr. Big comes back to tell us we're doing it all wrong."

He snatched the spoke from Finn's hand and shoved it around. It went almost of its own accord, because that was the way *Anadyomene* wanted to go, down the steep rails. The wheels of the trolley groaned like a sluggard waking from long sleep. Emma turned to watch the brightness of the water change its shape as the fattening curve of the hull bulked between the doorposts. The groaning raised its pitch and the knock of the turning cogs quickened and quickened again.

"Ouch!" yelled Roddy. Emma spun round and saw him sucking at the knuckles of his right hand while with his left he tried to catch one of the whirling spokes. Anna was now doing all the work, spinning the cogs around as she trundled unstoppably towards her element. The winch and rails rumbled and the shed thundered. Finn hovered behind Roddy and was just darting in to try and help him when one of the spokes spun clean out of its slot and crashed into the roof tiles. Finn snatched at Roddy's shoulder and dragged him back to the wall as another spoke hurtled out and bounced with a deep clang off the hull. Emma would have liked to run into the open, but she had been standing on the far side of the shed from the door and now didn't dare edge past the winch; all she could do was move further down towards the water.

Andy came racing into the shed with Ewan behind him. He picked up the fallen spoke and dodged around behind the winch; from Emma's side he leaned across the drum (still turning incredibly slowly — it was only the high-geared cogs which were whirling) and used the end of the spoke to flick the lug over and shove it against the cog. But the cog was moving too fast for it to fall between the teeth; it clattered for a moment and bounced back. Ewan Uphill picked a chock off the beam, waved it, and shouted to Andy.

"No!" yelled Andy. "Tip her off!" Probably Ewan couldn't even hear that across the shed, but he understood Andy's gesture and put the chock back. Andy flipped the lug up with the spoke again, and this time leaned his weight against it as it jolted onto the cog.

Suddenly everything changed. Emma heard three loud bangs from different parts of the shed, and felt the wind of something whistling close past her, just over her head. Then there was less noise, only the rumble of the trolley as *Anadyomene* rushed down towards the water. Emma hadn't even time to wonder why the trolley was now moving so much more quickly, or why the dull rattle of the winch had suddenly stopped, before the wheels touched the water. Even now *Anadyomene* was not moving tremendously fast — about ten miles an hour, perhaps — so the accidental launching happened slowly enough for her to watch the whole of it: how the first small ripples had begun to spread from the wheels before the bulk of the hull overwhelmed everything in a foaming wave which hummocked up on either side while the brilliant droplets of the huge splash

73

glittered up into the sunlight. Then the water pattered back over the green bronze while the submarine sank and sank until she rested, rocking, with only a foot or two of metal showing round the squat conning tower; it looked more like a bowler hat than ever now. The wave sloshed up the ramp beneath the rails, almost to Emma's feet, then slid back again.

"Zow-ee!" said Ewan Uphill, breaking the astonished quiet.

"Like a sow diving," said Roddy.

"Are you all right?" said Finn. It was several seconds before Emma realized that Finn was talking to her.

"Yes," she said, looking around. "What happened?"

There was a whole plank missing from the wall of the shed behind her. Through it, still twitching slightly, like a recently shot snake, ran the cable which a minute before had been taut under the weight of the submarine.

"I'm an idiot," said Andy, quiet and rather white-faced. "I should have let her run. What happened, Cousin Emma, was that I got the locking lug back into the cog and that stopped the winch dead and the extra strain snapped the cable. When you snap a taut steel cable it lashes sideways hard enough to . . . anyway, hard enough to knock a good oak plank clean out of the wall. But it missed you, and that's what matters."

"It was my fault," said Finn. "I should have realized Roddy wasn't strong enough to hold her. The spokes started turning too fast for him. What shall we do now?"

They all looked out at the absurd metal bowler, lying stolid in the settling water.

"Poop's going to have to do some swimming," said Andy.

They found Miss Newcombe out in the sunlight, lolling

74

against the tractor in a way that made her absurd dressing gown and the brutal blue metal and the steep slope of young pines in the background look all perfectly natural — not like a glossy advertisement, thought Emma, like part of Eden.

"That was lovely," she said. "Can we all go for a ride now?"

"You can go for a swim now," said Andy. "The exercise didn't work out exactly as we intended."

"I was wondering," said Miss Newcombe. "It seemed a funny way to do things."

She pointed to where the loose end of cable hung with its snapped shackle out of the gash in the boathouse wall, a still snake now.

"We won't try to repeat that effect," said Finn. "She'll never be able to swim with the logging cable, Andy. Couldn't Roddy row you out there and you can use the engine to bring Anna back."

"No dice," said Andy. "No one's going aboard her till she's hitched up to Ewan's tractor. If we buoy the cable Poop can swim with it easily enough."

"What about that spool of nylon rope in the long boat-house?" said Roddy. "That'd be quicker."

He scampered off without waiting for an answer and came back with a spool of shiny orange rope.

"Good-oh," said Andy. "What knots do you know, Poop?"

"I can tie a bow. I don't think I can tie anything else. People in post offices always do my parcels up again for me. They say they'll come undone."

"Oh, God," said Andy.

"A bow will do fine," said Finn. "Make it a double one,

75

like you do when you don't want your shoelaces to come undone. Where'd she better tie it, Andy?"

"On the shackle just under the point of the bow. That's a sort of iron loop, Poop, this end, about four feet under water. Don't try and tie it anywhere else — we can't afford to have her tilting around, because the hatch isn't fastened."

Miss Newcombe tossed her dressing gown on the grass, put the end of the rope between her teeth, stepped without a tremor into the water, turned on her back, and began a lazy backstroke out towards the bowler hat. Roddy unreeled the cable as she went.

"Doesn't it get deep quickly?" said Emma. "She was only a yard out before she had to start swimming."

"It's not as steep here as it is in some places," said Roddy. "The burn's washed enough stuff down from the hillside to make a sort of shelf; but further out you get these underwater cliffs — I told you — and they go *straight* down. It's like Loch Morar. Nobody knows how deep that is, either."

"And nobody kens what's in those deeps, indeed," said Ewan Uphill. "When I was a bairn I would give myself the nightmare, wondering what swam down there in the unholy dark."

Emma shivered.

"That's like the words on Darwin's Pimple," she said. "The dark abysm."

"That's from *The Tempest*," said Finn. "Tiresome old Prospero talking about time — the dark backward and abysm of time."

"She's there," said Roddy.

They all watched in silence as the white bathing cap

76

flipped itself under, smoothly, like a seal. Emma started to count the seconds; at forty-two the bathing cap appeared again.

"Finished?" called Andy.

"No," came the faintly gasping reply.

Next time she was under for less than thirty seconds, and waved a triumphant arm.

"Hardly worth hitching her to the tractor," said Andy. "We can tow her around by hand."

It seemed an impossible suggestion to Emma that five people, two of them children, should haul the big hulk through the water, and indeed the first minute was a tug-of-war, with their heels slipping on the sparse turf and the orange curve of the rope rising right out of the water except for the last few feet, dripping along its length, and then falling back with a slap as somebody lost his footing and the tension eased. But suddenly the feel of the rope changed, there was different grass underfoot and *Anadyomene* was swinging through the water.

"Easy, easy!" said Andy and dashed for the further boathouse. The rope slackened, but *Anadyomene* continued to drift towards the shore. Andy came back with a long, varnished pole — a spare mast for the dinghy.

"Keep her moving," he said.

So in slow swoops, sometimes all hauling on the rope, sometimes resting and watching while Andy and Ewan poled the hidden hull away from the rocks, they maneuvered the submarine along the shore, out around the rough jetty and back towards the slipway. All the time Miss Newcombe gamboled and splashed about as though *Anadyomene* were some huge beach toy, laughing and gasping and getting in the way. Not until they had the hull nestling against the jetty did she climb out and scamper for her towel and dressing gown.

"It's not like the photographs," said Finn.

"What do you mean?" said Andy.

"We've got Mother's Coronation Year pictures in one of the old albums. You could see much more of the hull, I think. And there'd have been Father and Andy Coaches aboard to weigh her down."

"And stones for ballast," said Emma. "You said they had trouble getting her under at all."

"Um," said Andy. "Perhaps the ballast tanks flooded a bit in that splash. That'd make sense. But don't worry — we'll be all right on the end of Ewan's cable. Where d'you want to dig in, Ewan? There's rock at the top of the slip-way."

"Aȳe," said Ewan, "that'll not do. And there's a wee bit bog behind, and that'll not do either. I'll try her a step or two up the hill."

"Right," said Andy, stripping off his shirt and kilt and lowering himself into the water in his bathing trunks. Ewan lounged off. Andy forced himself clumsily under the water, and in a few seconds came up gasping. Next time he stayed down longer. Emma was surprised to see that he was nothing like so good a swimmer as Miss Newcombe, despite a lifetime spent by the loch, but didn't like to say so. Sleek with water the black head plopped into view.

"We've pulled Poop's knot so tight I'll have to cut it," Andy panted. "Borrow your knife, Roddy?"

They heard a cry from up the hill. Ewan was waving as though he wanted help. Finn stared shorewards along the jetty and Emma went with her.

"Is the feud over?" she said as soon as they were out of earshot.

"Hope so," said Finn. "It was nearly killing you that did it, and then all that heaving and shoving before they had time to start blaming each other."

"You took the blame," said Emma.

Finn smiled her curious smile, as though nobody else saw the jokes she saw.

"We're all liars," she said. "I just like to keep in practice."

Ewan was literally digging, with a spade, a short deep trench just behind where the tractor faced uphill. Emma saw that when he had finished it the winch could be lowered until a shovellike blade below would exactly fit into the trench; then the winch would have not just the weight of the tractor to hold it steady but the solid earth as well.

"That's grand," said Ewan. "You can just kindly lug the cable down for me and tell Mr. Andy I'll be ready as soon as he is. No, wrap a bit of rag round it, Miss Emma; cable's cruel stuff for soft hands."

The winch drum turned easily as they hauled the cable downhill. The cable had a heavy D-shaped clip at the end of it, which Andy took and dived in with; its weight helped him down and he fastened it first go, then climbed out onto the jetty and dried himself roughly while Emma looked tactfully up the melodramatic reaches of the loch, far and shimmering beyond where the harsh diagonal of pines plunged to the water.

"That's the shallow end, isn't it?" she said.

"It's not a swimming pool," said Andy.

"But it is very different, isn't it?" said Finn. "I mean it's almost as though we had two lochs, with bags of fish and

79

weed up there and nothing but a few cunning trout down here. There's even a scientific name for the two sorts of lake, but I always forget it."

"That end's eutrophic," said Andy. "This end's oligo-trophic. If it's Greek to you, that's because it *is* Greek. Hi, Poop, where've you been? That was some knot you tied."

"I don't like wearing wet swimsuits. What are you going to do now?"

"I'll nip aboard, shut the hatch, check that the light's working and that there aren't any leaks, and try and find out why she's lying so low. If everything looks shipshape, we'll try taking her out a bit further. Hang on to that end of the ladder, Roddy."

He placed the short ladder they had been using in the boathouse out onto the hull beside the conning tower, so that it became a sort of skeleton bridge from the jetty. Roddy steadied the jetty end and Andy spidered out until he could place his feet on either side of the conning tower. Carefully he worked himself upright until he stood teeter-ing on the rocking hull. His weight drove it deeper, so that now the water lapped right against the conning tower, just below the two glass windows. Still moving like a tightrope-walker in a circus, he gently eased the hatch open and low-ered himself inside. The hatch closed, then clicked. They waited in the sunlight. Roddy, itching for action, suddenly rushed up the hill to talk to Ewan. Eight feet along the jetty the water rumbled as though a big fish were strug-gling in a net just below the surface; slowly the conning tower edged out towards the loch and the logging cable rat-tled a little as it slipped over the cement of the slipway. The churning settled and began again, and the conning tower drifted back towards the shore, stopped almost where they were standing, and then, after a fresh swirl, edged out a couple of feet again. The hatch rose and Andy's head came out, grinning.

"No trouble," he said. "I touched bottom when I came back in. That motor runs like a dream. Do you feel like taking the risk, Finn?"

"Roddy would love to go first."

"No dice. I don't feel like depriving Father of all his male issue in one morning. I think we're OK, but this *is* a dangerous toy, lovey."

"OK," said Finn, as though that made it much better.

"Right," said Andy. "Now listen, Emma. I want to take her out just clear of the jetty, so that I don't damage the hydroplanes if we come up in a different place from where we went down. We know how deep it is here, so if the slope goes on at this angle that should give us ten feet to the bottom. Lend her your watch, Finn. Allow five minutes after we've gone under, and if we don't show by then get Ewan to haul us in. Let me get settled, Finn, then come aboard. Step delicate, and if it looks like you're going to push the hatch under, jump into the loch."

He disappeared. Emma took Finn's watch and buckled the fat strap around her wrist, then held the ladder end. Finn stepped onto the rung and simply walked out, balancing easily. By the time she reached the conning tower it had sunk another five inches, covering the glass. Gingerly Finn lowered herself in. Again the hatch clanked shut, and after a short pause the silent churning of the propeller dragged the tower out along the jetty until it lay about ten yards beyond the end, like a buoy waiting for somebody to come along and moor to it. Even in this clear water the shimmer off the surface prevented her from seeing anything of the hull at all. Slowly the tower began to sink; it took two minutes to disappear completely. Emma looked at the watch: twenty to one.

"Typical," said Roddy, frowning beside her. She knew at once what he meant.

"Andy said it might be dangerous," she said, "and he didn't want to drown both the male McAndrews in one morning. Do you think it really is dangerous? I can't get used to the way you seem to rush in to things."

"I'm so glad," said Miss Newcombe. "Nor can I."

"Yes," said Roddy, his frown vanishing. "Yes, that would be hell on Finn."

"What would?"

"If Roddy and I were killed, she'd become Clan Chief when Father dies; and then she'd pretty well have to marry one of the Fertagh McAndrews. They're drips."

It seemed one of the oddest arguments Emma had ever heard for allowing oneself to be drowned in a bronze trap, but it seemed to have stilled Roddy's wrath for a bit, so she said nothing. She looked at the watch: eighteen minutes to one. The seconds ached away. No ripple troubled the water.

"Hello," said Roddy. "They're going further out."

He pointed at the cable and Emma saw that it was inching along the concrete.

"But they haven't got the propeller going," she said. "We'd have seen that boiling it makes."

"Did he say how deep he was going?"

"About ten feet. That wouldn't pull the cable out — not that much. Roddy —"

But Roddy spun round, waved an urgent arm at Ewan, and shouted. The distant knock of the tractor engine quickened and deepened. The cable rattled back up the slipway and rose clear until it ran almost straight from the winch to the top edge of the concrete, touched there, and ran straight down to the water. Once it was taut it didn't budge an inch inland. The tractor gave a brief roar and Emma saw its front wheels buck slightly at the extra strain.

"He mustn't do that," said Roddy and raced up the hill. Yes, thought Emma, a jerk like that might simply tear the bows out.

"What's happening, darling?" said Miss Newcombe's voice, slightly anxious. "Is something, er, wrong?"

"I think they're stuck out there, under the water. The tractor can't pull them in. Perhaps they're wedged under an old cable or something."

"Shall I go and see?" said Miss Newcombe. She dropped her dressing gown idly on the jetty and ran down the far end, changing her springy pace at the last instant so that she took off perfectly for an almost splashless dive, and was gone too. Emma began to count the seconds, finding it hard to keep the count steady against the heavy banging of her heart. Fifty-one, and the blond head shot up, gasping, fifteen yards out; she didn't dive again but came back to the jetty at a quick crawl.

"Too deep," she panted. "I found the rope thing, but it goes over a sort of edge, and just . . . down."

"You couldn't see Anna?"

"No."

"How far out is the cliff edge?"

"A bit . . . nearer than where . . . I came up."

Emma raced up the hill towards the tractor, meeting Roddy who was hurrying down, but she plunged on to where Ewan sat frowning and gasped the news to him. He fiddled with the controls of the tractor so that the winch turned twice and the cable lay slack along the grass, then the three of them walked down to the jetty where Miss Newcombe stood biting her knuckles.

"Yess," said Ewan. "It's stuck under something they are."

"I think I could go deeper . . . now I know where to look," said Miss Newcombe.

"No," said Ewan. "They'll do for a wee while. There's no real weight there, not while she's in the water. No bubbles you saw, Miss Poop?"

"Bubbles? No."

"Then they'll have air now, for a little. I'd best be taking my bike up to Andy Ghillie's, and then we'll have four men about. It'll be a matter of rigging a big float — barrels, all lashed — Master Roddy, if you'd be going to tell Andy Coaches to find what he can in the buildings — and I've got some long timbers back of the hill there — I'll bring them down with the other tractor — and we can spar the float out beyond this cliff place and maybe pull the submarine outwards, see? And if that dinna serve —"

"Look, look!" shouted Roddy. "They're going deeper."

The cable was once more grating across the slipway.

"I locked the winch — I'm hoping," said Ewan and began to race up the hill.

Despairing, Emma watched the cable shift and shift, three feet, four. It stopped for an instant, straight along the slipway but not truly taut, then all at once it gave a little wriggle and lost its straightness — whatever had been pulling it was pulling no longer.

"The bows have broken," whispered Emma.

She snatched her gaze out across the water to see the

84

huge bubble rise, the bubble that would mean the end of proud, fierce Andy, and of Finn, whom Emma had liked more than anybody she had ever met, or ever would meet.

The water boiled and creamed.

No bubble could be that shape, nor that hard and gray, like a flattish bowler hat rocking amid the turbulence.

The waves settled and there lay *Anadyomene,* a foot further out of the water than she had been even before Andy had first got into her, with almost three feet of the hull showing fore and aft.

"Oh, super!" said Miss Newcombe. "Wasn't that horrid! And I've ruined my hair, too."

They heard a shout from up the hill and the changed note of the tractor engine. The cable rattled along the slipway; Roddy ran for the spar to pole the submarine clear of the jetty, but Ewan judged his job so neatly that soon the green hull was lying just where it had been in the clear water by the knobbly planking. The hatch hinged open and Finn climbed out, her face gray-white like oatmeal, her glorious hair drenched. No proud balancing along the ladder this time; instead she crawled ashore, where Miss Newcombe put an arm round her shoulder, as much to be comforted as to comfort her. Nobody said anything until Andy, also dripping wet, was safe on the jetty.

"What happened?" said Roddy. "What went wrong? You were stuck over the cliff, and Poop couldn't go any deeper. Why are you wet?"

"I don't know what happened," said Andy.

"We're wet because the windows leaked," said Finn.

"It wasn't much," said Andy. "A few squirts where the rubber seal around the windows had rotted. Two or three cupfuls."

"We couldn't *see!*" said Finn.

"Yes," said Andy. "That was the trouble."

"Why did you go so deep?" said Emma.

"We didn't mean to. I think the ballast tanks must have been quite empty on the trolley, and stayed empty after the launching. We flooded them a bit to sink, and overdid it, and then the pumps wouldn't empty them completely so we were still not quite buoyant and just went on sinking. That pressure gauge registers all right. Then the seals gave way and started spouting, and then one of you must have spotted that something was wrong, because Ewan started to haul us in before the five minutes were up —"

"That was Roddy," said Emma quickly.

"— only of course our tail was still sinking and we started to tilt and then he hauled us in under something — our nose, that is — but the tail went on going down. I had to drag Finn right up to the bows, and that was just enough to even the weight out, so we sat there . . ."

"Listening to the loch hissing in," said Finn.

"Yes. Then Finn remembered this handle she'd seen, and we thought we might as well give it a try."

"I saw it yesterday," said Finn. "I thought it was just something for the crew to steady themselves by, but it said 'Weight Release'."

"Yes, I saw that," said Emma. " 'Weight Release' and an arrow to show you which way to turn it. I didn't know what it meant."

"It meant that Grandfather had fitted a safety device," said Andy. "Or Monsieur Goubet, perhaps. You were right, Cousin Emma — we damned near sank Anna with the weight of the extra batteries. Father had run her in

Coronation Year without the safety weight, which is why he'd had to add ballast to get her under at all . . ."

"What sort of safety weight?" said Roddy. "How did it work?"

"I imagine it was a great lump of lead under the keel, with this release shaft screwed down into it. We turned and turned it, and nothing happened, and then it must have screwed itself free because we were bucketing all over the place as the nose came out from whatever we were stuck under, and up we shot and saw daylight."

"I see," said Roddy. "It's just like chucking ballast out of a balloon. Dead cunning, these Victorians. I wonder what's for lunch."

Over lunch Andy said, "It's not as bad as it might be, unless the trolley has gone over the cliff too. But there's probably some kind of stop on the rails. If Poop will be kind enough to nip down and survey the damage, then we can haul the trolley up, get Anna ashore, and rig her up with a lighter weight. There's tons of lead in Big House."

"What about the windows?" said Finn.

"Plastic cement should fix those, and . . ."

Emma listened horrified. She could have understood if it had been only Roddy, but Andy and Finn were grown up, or almost. When there was a pause she broke in, a little shrilly.

"You don't mean you're going on with it?" she said. "After this morning?"

"We can't stop now!" said Roddy, fiercely.

"We've only been a bit unlucky," said Finn.

"You mean you've been frightfully lucky," said Emma.

87

"You only just didn't kill yourselves; you only just didn't kill me, and —"

"My dear Cousin Emma," said Andy loftily. "You are doing me an injustice. In fact we are behaving very carefully and sensibly, taking every possible precaution. That's why I propose to go to the trouble of making a new safety weight from the lead pipes at Big House — because I don't want to run any unnecessary risks. It's typical of Father that he went barging about the loch in Coronation Year with no safety weight at all. That's what I call dangerous."

"Father's an ass," said Roddy.

"No he isn't," said Miss Newcombe. "He's cleverer than everyone else put together."

"I know that," said Roddy. "But he's an ass, too."

5

"Yesterday was rather boring," wrote Emma
twelve days later. As usual, she clicked her pen
against her teeth and looked out over the loch; it
looked rather boring, too — or perhaps it was just
her mood, for quite a lot of things had happened
yesterday, only she didn't feel like writing about
them. She and Ewan had done one perfect run
across the loch, judging both depth and distance
right; then they'd driven off to picnic on the des-
olate slopes of Ben Goig, spent a lounging after-
noon in the dinghy catching enough of the
hungry little trout that swarmed at the shallow
end to make a luscious supper, and while Emma
and Finn and Caitlin, the cook, had been shelling
young peas in the evening Caitlin had told them

*the most marvelous ghost story, not frightening at
all, but weird and beautiful. But Emma didn't
feel like writing about any of that. Even the
young deer which she and Roddy had surprised
when they stalked up a ridge in the hope of
spotting some of the wildcats which no one ever
saw by day but which miaowed so often in the
dark — she didn't even feel like writing about
how the deer had stared at them, shocked, for
one eternal instant before bounding away, zig-
zagging down the slope. Though that was just the
sort of thing Miss Sturmer would like.*

*It was waiting to hear from the television peo-
ple that made everything else seem monotonous.
Never mind, she thought. Perhaps she was writing too much. Fifty-seven pages was an awful lot
to expect anyone to read, even eager Miss Sturmer.*

*The thought made a good excuse to leaf back
and read what she'd written before, and look
again at the photographs. She wished she dared
ask Finn to take a close-up of Miss Newcombe;
but having the photographs at all was a stroke of
luck. And cunning.*

The two girls were putting another layer of fiber onto
the monster's head. The pear-drop reek of the resin suddenly made Emma feel ill, and she ran for the open doors
at the water's edge and stood there, gasping for sweet air.
Both girls had rushed out of the boathouse like this several
times, so Finn hardly looked up from her work, busy with

the task of rolling a whole layer into shape before the resin started to set.

It was a dullish day, heavy, with many insects darting through the moist, warm, motionless air. The worst of them were the horseflies, which had settled and sucked and stung before you even noticed the tickle of them. It was because they didn't come into the boathouse that the girls were enduring the appalling resin smell.

Out across the leaden water a motor launch was moving; the faint puck-puck of its engine was the only noise she could hear until Ewan Uphill's chain saw, somewhere up in the plantations, ripped the morning apart. The boys were leaning over the back of the launch, studying the behavior of the monster's tail; from the shore Emma could see that it was getting much more lifelike. The early experiments with tractor tires had looked like nothing except tractor tires; and when Andy had filled them with enough water to show only a couple of little hummocks above the surface they had become more than *Anadyomene* would conceivably tow. The latest tail was much more streamlined — a plastic heating duct discarded by the kippering factory at Mallaig, with bits added. The first two thirds of it were very convincing, but the back needed further adjustments.

"Finn," said Emma.

"Yes, you needn't come back. I'm just finishing."

"Where's your camera?"

"In The Huts."

"I think you ought to take a few photographs."

"What of?"

"Things like the head, before it's painted. And the boys with the tail behind the launch. And Anna, of course."

"Why?"

"Well . . . I thought . . . well, it's just possible that you might need to prove that the whole thing's a fake. I mean, if it got out of hand. I mean, I know you all enjoy lying, but it's useful to be able to prove the truth."

Finn smiled to herself and went on rolling the resin into the curves of her beast; it looked better with every layer of fiber glass, less heraldic, meaner, more like a thing that has grown and not simply been manufactured. Some layers had made it look suddenly drunk, but this one was going well, with the tiny head just the right proportions for the short, arching neck. Finn had wanted a longer neck, but Andy had insisted that it would drag too much in the water, so she'd had to make it stubby, and spreading enough at the shoulders to cover the whole conning tower; now it looked clumsy, but clumsy in a natural way. Emma thought of the ugly weight of a rhinoceros — Finn's beast would have something of that quality, when it was done.

"That'll do," said the sculptress, standing up and stepping back. "Let's hope Andy says it's strong enough. I'll get the camera."

Emma lolled and slapped horseflies as they settled, and watched the boys. By the time Finn came back with her equipment they had stopped the motor and were hauling the tail alongside for Andy to fiddle with. Finn stood in the shadow of the doorway and clicked her lens; like a proper photographer she took twenty times as many pictures as she could possibly use — but she could afford to because she did her own developing, using the old laboratory, the oldest part of The Huts, as a darkroom. When she had used up three rolls of film they strolled back there, lax in the oppressive air. Miss Newcombe was sitting on the verandah

92

writing with immense and frowning concentration her weekly letter to Major McAndrew. Andy had rigged a mosquito netting for her, and she sat under this with a very old typewriter on her lap, choosing the letters one by one and hitting them like enemies. The day after Andy and Finn had nearly drowned, Emma had looked at the letter Miss Newcombe was writing then; it was quite short, in two paragraphs. The first one said that the writer was well, and how much she weighed, and that the weather was fine and they might go for a picnic. The second was longer, and started with questions about what the weather in Geneva was like and whether Major McAndrew was taking his vitamin pills and was he sleeping any better; then it reminded him not to eat any lobsters because they made him sick; then it hoped that Swiss women were all very ugly but said Miss Newcombe had seen a TV program about a place which she thought was either Switzerland or Sweden but anyway some of the girls looked just his type and would he please think about beetles and nothing else. Nothing about the drowning. Emma had felt ashamed of her peeping. Now the girls crept past so as not to spoil Miss Newcombe's concentration.

The laboratory was a lovely room, a sort of tidy jumble. Glass-fronted cupboards held old brass apparatus and bits of experiments and strange-shaped glass jars and tubes. Apart from Finn's photographic kit all the things in the room were at least fifty years old and made, like *Anadyomene,* as well as possible; the cupboard doors and the shutters to darken the windows hissed slightly as you closed them, so cleanly did they fit. A huge safe squatted in one corner.

While Finn still had the lights on and was fiddling with

her bottles of developer, Emma carried on with her self-appointed job of looking for the two missing volumes of her great-grandfather's diaries.

The evening after the near-drowning the feud between Andy and Roddy had almost broken out again. Andy had a pencil and paper on his knee and was muttering away at sums about how much lead piping he would have to tear out of Big House and hammer into shape to provide a new safety weight for *Anadyomene*.

Suddenly Roddy said "Father knew. So *we* ought to have known."

Andy said nothing, and Roddy was just beginning to look really angry when Finn said "You'll have to explain. It sounds like a riddle."

"Father took the weight off to run her in Coronation Year," said Roddy. "Therefore he knew there was a weight to take off. Therefore we should have known."

"That's not logic," said Andy. "You've got an undistributed middle there, or something."

"An undistributed riddle," said Finn.

"It'll be in Grandfather's diaries, of course," said Roddy. "The whole design, everything. He won't have left out something like Anna. You ought to have looked."

"I did look," said Andy coldly. "That volume's missing. Father must have fished it out for his Coronation stunt and put it back in the wrong place. Or lent it to somebody and forgot to ask for it back."

"Of course it's there!" shouted Roddy. "They all are!"

"I always thought they were," said Finn. "There isn't a gap."

"Go and look," said Andy, and threw his leg over the side of his armchair to show he had no intention of going with them. "You can waste your time if you like."

He lit one of his sweet-smelling cheroots, picked up *The Scotsman,* which never arrived until six o'clock, and screened himself with it from his family's idiocies. The others went to the laboratory and found that he was right. But while they had been desultorily searching the other bookshelves, Emma had noticed Miss Newcombe's reflection in one of the glass cupboard doors. She was standing by one of the workbenches and had lifted a flat brown box off the shelf behind it; she opened the lid and stared inside; her lithe hand leaped forward, picked something out, and leaped back again; then, slowly and casually, she put the box back on the shelf and bent to adjust her shoe; when she straightened up she held her hands in such a way that you could see there was nothing in them. Emma had told Finn about it when Roddy and Miss Newcombe left the room. Finn had laughed, fetched the box down, and opened it. On purple velvet, each in its own circular nest, lay row after row of lenses, gleaming like jewels. One was missing.

"Poop likes to keep in practice too," Finn had said. "It's all right; Jeannie will find it when she cleans Poop's room and give it to Mary and Mary will give it to me. But it's useful to know where it belongs. I wonder what on earth happened to those diaries — I'm sure Father would have put them back — he's very pernicketty. And Poop wouldn't have nicked *books.*"

So now Emma was working her way along the shelves which covered the whole of the far end of the room. They had been built to house deep tomes, and where they held smaller books there was sometimes another row of books behind, and usually at least a gap down which a volume might have fallen; so Emma was working systematically from the top left corner, cleaning the tops of all the books with the little hand vacuum as she went, so as not to stir up dust and ruin Finn's processes. She looked at every book, though three-quarters of them were in foreign languages, and yesterday she had found trove—a little French pamphlet in which M. Goubet had described the design and operation of his submarine. Andy had been pleased, though it turned out that Grandfather had changed a great many devices; *Goubet I,* for instance, had had no hydroplanes or fins, and it had had electric pumps for the ballast tanks, while *Anadyomene* had hand pumps; and storage bottles for air, and an extraordinarily complicated system for balancing fore and aft by pumping water to and fro, which *Anadyomene* didn't need because her hydroplanes made her more maneuverable. She had a bigger engine than *Goubet I,* too, though Andy said it would use up her batteries much faster — but then there was only the loch to explore, whereas *Goubet I* had been built to operate in the open sea. So the pamphlet was not as much use as it might have been, and Emma went on searching for the diaries.

She had reached the third of the second column of shelves when Finn said "Lights out. This'll take about three minutes." So there was nothing to do except sit in the dark on the little mahogany stepladder and listen to the rustle of Finn threading the spools of film into the developing tanks.

"Is the feud over?" said Emma.

"It looks like it, but we grow very long memories up here."

"Yes. Andy told me all about Glencoe in the car, as if it still mattered."

"Oh, *that* matters. I know people still who'll have no truck with a Campbell."

"But Roddy and Andy?"

"I don't know. It depends. While there's amusing work to be done it should be OK, and then if Gabriella comes, and if she's nice to him . . . but until then he's bound to feel edgy, and Roddy's bound to take advantage. Lights on."

Emma blinked and climbed back to her shelves while Finn poured the developer into the first tank and set the timer; then she came over and watched Emma working.

"What's Gabriella like?" asked Emma.

"Fat. Dark, curly hair. A bit gypsyish. Laughs a lot. Not pretty, but interesting. You mustn't get the idea that Andy's actually besotted with her. He'd just got bored of a stunning actress with no manners and no sense of humor when he first met Gabriella, and she was a change. A very nice change for *us,* I may say. She came and stayed for a bit, and then she went back to her job — that was last holidays. Andy expected her to run to and fro when he wanted her — he's used to the little dollies at Edinburgh being bowled over by his looks and money and style — I mean, he's fun to be with when he's in the mood, isn't he? But he couldn't do that with Gabriella, who's very much her own person — rather like you are, in that way — and I think he got the idea that she thought he wasn't, well, *grown up* enough for her, with her job on TV and her slick friends. I

97

mean Andy's brainy, but in some lights he's still a bit of a country cousin. Anyway he wants to see her again partly because he likes her, but partly he wants to pull a very fast one on her TV friends and the whole setup, in front of her, to show them where *they* get off."

"I hope none of you ever get your knife into the Tuppers."

"Oh, you're blood kin. Besides, *you* can look after yourself."

Ping went the timer, and Finn moved back to the sink and poured liquids about while Emma thought how strangely different you seem to be from outside compared with what you know you are inside. It was twenty minutes before the first film came dripping out of the hypo and Finn was able to hold it up to the light and see what she'd got. Emma came and peered at the negatives, loch and hills all white and the launch a black blob in the middle.

"This bit'll blow up quite nicely," said Finn. "Look, you can see a lot of the tube there, with Roddy holding it steady for Andy, and you can see this other bit in the water looking quite monsterish. I'll have to use the telephoto for the movie camera, or nothing will show. It's always astonishing how close you have to get to things."

"Can you develop the movie film yourself?"

"I've got the kit. Mother gave it me last Christmas, but it's trickier than this and sometimes I make a botch. If we can do several runs with the boat I'll see what I can get out of a couple of them; then, if they're no good, we'll have to send the others away. I don't want to do that, because it will leave longer for the boys to go sour again."

Emma picked Finn's rectangular magnifying glass off the bench and peered through it at the strip of film.

98

"You wouldn't think they'd been having a feud," she said.

"No. But even if I do get a decent strip of action developed and we send it off to Gabriella's boss, it'll be several days before we hear anything. Andy's going to be as edgy as hell."

"We'd better reserve our peace-keeping energies till then."

"*You* can. I'm just a neutral. Women are the Third World in this house, but if you want to be a one-girl UN observer corps, good luck to you."

"I'll wait and see."

Emma didn't have to wait long. They came in late to supper, triumphant with having fitted the painted head to the conning tower and the tail to the stern of *Anadyomene*. When the big gong boomed in the hall to call them to the dining room, she was still trying to remove the last of the appalling fiber-glass resin from her fingers, so she never saw how the feud caught fire again, but she heard the angry yells crackling along the corridor and waited till they subsided.

By the time she reached the dining room Roddy had vanished, Mary was taking a tray loaded with one supper out of the further door, and Andy was sitting in his place, his cheeks blotchy with fury.

And he was furious again next morning with Roddy, who over his kippers announced in a careless voice that he was not going to help any more, in any way, with the monster project. The male McAndrews yelled and hissed at each other while the females ate in silence.

"Finn can do it," said Roddy.

"Oh, yes, and take telephoto movie films from the shore at the same time. And if the telly folk come, Gabby's sure to miss her."

"Ewan."

"Oh, for God's sake, he's already doing it. We need *two!*"

"Poop."

"Yes, darling," said Miss Newcombe.

"No, darling," said Andy.

It was the first time that Emma had heard anyone in that house speak even faintly unkindly to Miss Newcombe. Her longing to shut the stupid feud out of her mind made her slow to notice the silence and see that Finn and Andy were looking at her, while Roddy was looking carefully away. She caught Finn's eye and saw the faintest nodding of the long pale face.

"I'll be crew, if you like," she said. The very idea was a nightmare. Even on land, being inside the hull of *Anadyomene* felt like being in a dungeon. And to be trapped in that bronze bubble below the surface of the loch, with the unknown deeps beneath . . .

"What do you weigh?" said Andy brusquely.

"I don't know."

"Don't you really?" said Miss Newcombe, wide-eyed. "But you can use my scales — they're *very* accurate."

"Never mind," said Andy. "She'll be about right. She's lighter than Roddy but Ewan's heavier than I am. We can get along without you, Roddy, if that's how you want it."

"That's how," said Roddy.

No thanks from anybody. They probably didn't realize, *couldn't* realize . . .

In fact, the first trip was not as bad as Emma had feared. Andy was surprisingly considerate, now that he'd got his own way. The first thing Emma noticed after climbing out of the daylight was that Napoleon's nose had begun to tarnish.

"It didn't smell like this before," she said.

"Battery acid," said Andy. "They don't smell when you're using them, but they give off gas when they're recharging. I rigged that fan to clear it, but there's still a bit hanging about. Now, Cousin Emma, I'm going to have to tell you how this ship works. I may tell you things you already know, but don't stop me, or I might leave something important out which you don't know. But for heaven's sake stop me if there's anything you don't understand. Right?"

Emma nodded.

"Good girl. Well, a submarine is a tin can which weighs almost as much as the same volume of water, so it *just* floats. Underneath, it has ballast tanks, which you can let more water into. In Anna there are four tanks, and you flood them by turning these two stopcocks here and these two at the back. When you do that, you let the air in the tank come up into the hull; it's pushed there by the pressure of the water outside, but the water can't come right up and flood the hull because the air pressure in the hull rises as the tanks fill until it's equal to the water pressure outside. Now, you see, the hull will weigh almost exactly the same as the water. If you let a cupful more into the tanks you will sink; a cupful less and you will bob up. It's almost impossible to get it so that you don't go up or down. In Anna we try to get it so that we're just going up."

"How can you tell what you're doing once the window is underwater?"

"Depth gauge here. It works by water pressure and seems quite accurate. And you tell whether you're lying level with this gauge here, which works just like a spirit level."

"Why's the pressure gauge by the front seat and the level by the back seat?"

"That's where you come in, Cousin Emma. We've got Anna barely floating, so we start the motor. Go and sit in the back seat."

Emma settled onto the old, crackly black leather.

"Comfortable?" said Andy.

"I'm not tall enough to see out."

"You wouldn't be able to anyway with the beast's head in position. Right, you've got two controls there —"

"These two gear lever sort of things?"

"Yes, except that you'll find they don't waggle from side to side, they just move to and fro. Hang on while I disconnect the motor. OK, now, that one on your left is the motor control. It makes a bit of a spark when it engages, but it's quite easy to move. You pull it slightly sideways out of those notches and then it slides backwards and forwards and fits into the other notches, depending how fast you want the motor to run. Push it towards the tail, and we go backwards, pull it towards the bows and we go forwards. Try it."

Emma moved the ebony-handled truncheon to and fro in its groove. As Andy said, it slipped easily into the notches.

"Now," said Andy, "there is one absolute rule, Medes-and-Persians stuff. If the motor is going one way and you want it to go the other, you absolutely must wait until it's stopped turning. If you don't, you'll burn the whole thing out. You're going forward, and some ass of a captain tells you to go into reverse. You shove the lever to neutral, and wait. Wait. Never mind if he calls you beastly names, you wait until the motor's stopped turning, and *then* you obey. Got it?"

"Yes."

"Good girl. As a matter of fact you shouldn't have any need to reverse at all, even if you get in a jam, because you'd nearly certainly tangle the tail in the propeller; but I'd better tell you, just in case. Let's get on. We're submerged, and we're chugging along with just the top of the conning tower showing; the next thing to do is to get up speed. This boat is a sow at all times, but she's worse when she's going at speeds under one knot, because that's not fast enough for the hydroplanes to act on the water. If you try to go slower than that when you're submerged, you find that one moment you're standing on your nose and the next you're on your tail, so the thing is to get up speed while you're still roughly on the surface — it takes about a minute. Then we push her under. You do, rather. I give the word and you shove the hydroplane lever two notches away from you. The easiest way to think of the hydroplanes is as a sort of up-and-down rudder — you are *steering* us down, and the propeller pushes us further. Don't go more than four notches, or you'll steer the propeller into the tail. I steer with the propeller, which I can waggle in any direction I want, like an outboard motor, but I use it mostly for steering from side to side. Got all that?"

"Yes."

"Sure? It's a lot of technical stuff."

"It isn't difficult if you think about it."

"Aha! But we're coming to a bit that you won't be able to tackle with your mighty brain. That hydroplane lever was designed for a grown man to move, one-handed. You'll need both hands, and you'll find it pretty tough going even so. I told you Anna was a sow; well, part of her sowishness is that even when you're running level underwater she keeps trying to play the fool, skittering up and down all over the place. *Your* job is to keep your eye on that spirit level and use the hydroplanes to steady the hull. She has a tendency to want to get deeper, so we've been running her with the hydroplanes one notch up; but I shouldn't be surprised if the beast's head had much the same effect. We'll just have to see."

Emma put both hands around the ebony handle of the hydroplane lever, eased it out of the central notch, and pulled. She could feel the sluggish stirring of a big surface of metal trying to move through water.

"It's easy enough when we're lying still," said Andy. "Wait till you've got currents flowing over it. OK, let's give it a whirl. Motor in neutral while I connect up."

Emma pulled the motor control vertical and sat and looked around her while Andy fussed with cables. For the first time she noticed, clipped to the roof, a stubby pair of boat hooks. They seemed incongruous in the yellow light and the smell of battery acid — as though her great-grandfather had thought of *Anadyomene* as just another yacht. She wondered whether he wore a peaked yachting cap as he drove about underwater looking for his mythic monster.

Andy clucked to himself and sidled around Emma's chair to the steering seat. "Ready?" he said. "We'll run her gently out from the jetty on the surface, just to see how the tail drags. Motor half speed forward — shove it through — don't mind about the spark."

Flinchingly, Emma pulled at the black truncheon. A violet spark, three inches of lightning, leaped and crackled beside her feet, then stopped as she settled the lever into the middle of its forward arc. The motor groaned, hummed throatily, and rose to an easy tenor note as the submarine gained way and the effort to increase her speed through the water lessened.

"Try a bit more," said Andy. Emma pulled the lever almost to the last notch, and the hum rose to a whine. She felt the hull lurch slightly as Andy steered in a curve, and now she could hear the rattle of ripples against the hull, just beside her ears, surprisingly loud.

"OK," said Andy. "That's fine. She hardly notices it. Cut motor."

Again the spark leaped, the motor died and the ripple noise from outside seemed to become so loud that Emma for an instant was convinced that they were leaking and water was tinkling in to drown them. Then that noise stopped too as Anna drifted to stillness.

"Now we'll go down and see how the head behaves," said Andy. "Can you reach both stopcocks at once?"

"Yes, if I kneel on the floor."

"That'll do. When I say 'Now,' I want you to open both of them one full turn. Then I'll count from six down to zero, like a rocket blast-off, and at zero you shut them. Ready?"

"Yes," said Emma, kneeling on the cutting wooden slats of the deck and grasping the two metal rings that were the handles of the stopcocks.

"Now," said Andy.

Emma twisted the rings. Her left hand, always weaker than her right, was slower too. The faint tinkle of wavelets against the conning tower was drowned by a heavy gurgling below the decks, as though something was wrong with the plumbing. Her ears popped.

"Two. One. Zero," said Andy.

She wrenched the stopcocks shut. The yellow light was yellower now that honest day no longer came in though the little slit of glass and the carefully ragged hole that Finn had left at the base of the dragon's neck. Emma felt her throat begin to work as though she were trying to swallow something that wasn't there.

"Not bad," said Andy. "How's the level?"

Emma sat back in her chair and looked at the greenish-yellow liquid in the glass tube beside her armrest. The little bubble in it was halfway towards the front of the boat.

"We're down at the tail," she said. "Do you want to let more water in your end?"

"No. That would sink us. We're tilting a little to port, too. Try five strokes on your right-hand pump."

"My right or the boat's right? I'm facing backwards."

"*Your* right, I said." Andy sounded snappish for the first time. Emma crouched forward to the lever that rose beside the stopcock. A grown man could have worked it from the chair, but not Emma. The rod moved with surprising ease — less trouble than a bicycle pump — but she could sense the slight resistance of the water being driven out. After five strokes she craned back at the spirit level; now the bubble rested almost exactly between the two hairlines on the surface of the tube.

"Level," she said.

"OK. Motor two-thirds forward."

Again the violet lightning, again the rising note of the

106

engine. But this time a quite different noise from the hull — instead of the tinkling beside her ears a dull rattle above her head where the surface of the loch slid against fiber glass.

"Right," called Andy above the rising engine note. "When I say 'Now,' I want you to shove the hydroplane lever two notches away from you. Count ten, and then ease it back until the bubble's in the middle of the spirit level. After that you simply keep it there — don't think about anything else — and adjust the hydroplanes any way you want. Only tell me what you're doing. Ready? Now!"

Emma grunted as she felt the weight of water press the tilting surfaces outside, then slotted the lever home. She heard the rattle of the surface against the monster's neck dull, diminish and vanish. With a startling leap the bubble in the tube sidled towards the bows. She clicked the lever another notch back.

"We were going up," she shouted, "but we're level now."

"We're also back on the surface," said Andy. "Damn. It's that head. What we'll try now is this. Cut the motor two notches. Right. When I say 'Now,' use the hydroplane just like last time, but don't try to level off till we're a good ten feet under. I'll say when. Ready? Now!"

This time the bubble danced aft more slowly, and before Andy spoke, began to edge back towards its home in the middle of the tube.

"We're level," called Emma. "No we're not. We're going up."

She shoved the lever another notch along; the bubble steadied and sidled aft — too far.

"Now we're diving," she called, as she pulled the lever. "Shall I try to hold it between the notches?"

"No. We're fifteen feet under the porpoising. Try an extra notch of engine speed."

Fifteen feet under!

"That's better," said Emma. "But do you know where we are? Oughtn't we to go up and see? We might have been steering in circles."

Andy laughed.

"One point about a bronze hull is that it doesn't upset a compass," he said. "I've got the navigating compass from my Lotus just outside the window here. We're heading straight down the loch. But we'll go up and start again, once you're sure you know those lever positions. What we're going to have to do is run her under with hydroplanes sharply angled and ease back the moment we're under. Ready? Hydroplanes level. Back two notches. Up we go. Keep her going or the tail will come up and foul us. Great, here's daylight."

They tried diving and running under the surface several times before Andy was ready to do a timed run from known landmarks to see how fast *Anadyomene* was going underwater at the new speed. Emma's world became the strip of liquid in the tube, inhabited by one frail imp, a jigging bubble which she had to master with the clumsy lever. At each dive there was a hideous time when she had to hold the lever steady between two notches and in the next instant cut the engine speed. And at any moment, even when they were moving smooth and level, some quirk of the water or the hull would suddenly begin to tilt them and she had to catch the motion, correct and recorrect it until they settled back to sanity. The sudden upward surges she didn't mind — they were merely tiresome. But the plunges towards the deep filled her with panic, until her veins seemed to run with the same icy, lightless water that lay below her. Several times she glanced around to check the position of the weight-release wheel. Her lips began to mutter.

"What's that?" said Andy.

"The dark abysm," said Emma. "It's on Darwin's Pimple. I can't get it out of my mind."

"OK, we'll have a rest, then. You've done damn well, far better than Roddy. He can't concentrate — riding this thing with him was like being on a roller coaster. He'd have been OK on the day, of course. Let's go up and see if we can spot Finn — we might do a trial run for her to photograph. I wonder how much juice there is in those batteries — it's the stopping and starting they don't like. Ready? Hydroplanes neutral. Up. Motor to dead slow. Fine. Pumps."

Then there was a period while Emma sat in her seat and tried to relax by looking around at the absurd ornaments among the machinery and Andy stood with his shoulders out of the conning tower and halloed orders. Then again they shut out the day and dived.

"No talking," said Andy. "I've got to make timing and direction notes for Ewan. The only difference from the real thing is that we'll bob up for a bit before we do our main surfacing, so as to give Finn an idea about where to aim her camera. Ready for a slow turn to starboard. Now."

It made no difference to Emma, any more than the outside weather makes to a prisoner in a dungeon. She was still sitting in the bronze contraption, itself a bubble like the bubble in the spirit level, a bubble of breathable gas trapped by a cunning old Victorian under the killing waters. She wondered if any swimmer, even Miss Newcombe, would be able to escape supposing the bubble sprang a leak, collapsed, caved in. You'd have to take one great gulp of air — no, you'd have to wait, ready at the hatch, until the air was almost gone and the pressure outside and in was equal — gulp then, fumble the hatch open, endure the last rush of waters, and kick yourself free. And by then you'd be . . . how far down in the unholy dark? Ewan had called it that. And which way would be up? And . . .

"Stand by," said Andy. "We'll try popping up here."

Emma followed his brisk instructions. The light greened, grayed, became transfused with the slot of day invisible behind Emma's head, where Andy peered through the thick glass and the ragged edges of the hole which Finn had left in the beast's head.

"Where the hell are we?" he said. "Damn, we're a foot too far out — hydroplanes neutral — one notch back, that's better. Oh, I see, not at all bad, not at all bad. Ewan's going to have to practice surfacing. Now, down again."

Once more they sank. Once more they rose, and now Emma put the motor to full speed. This time Andy kept fiddling with his hydroplanes so that his visor slit was mostly below the surface, only edging clear for a second or two in every ten. Emma tried to follow him, as a girl might try to follow the steps of an erratic dancer; for almost two minutes the submarine surged along the surface at an awkward, plunging gait before Andy said, "Ready? Cut motor to underwater speed. Hydroplanes forward. Down. That's enough; try and hold it there. Now I'm going to try and take her back into the cove beyond the boathouses. I've done it without the head, so we'll just have to make allowances."

Emma sat managing her imp. She was beginning to know its ways now. She wondered what that other McAndrew had made of his job — the one who had had to sit in this chair while the old scientist chuntered around the loch. Was he frightened too? Or was the Chief, the McAndrew, then held in such awe that no whim of his, however wild, was questioned? Were the orders snapped in Gaelic? She made a sudden decision to get Caitlin to teach her some Gaelic. Could you take A-levels in Gaelic? Could you take them in Setsuana? It'd be fun to be the only girl in England doing both.

"Turning now," said Andy. "Motor to dead slow. Hydroplanes two notches forward — we don't want to hit anything, but we've got to keep her under till we're out of sight. Damn this compass. Settle down, will you! Hydroplanes back! Right back! Pumps!"

The sudden urgency brought all Emma's panic streaming back. She hurled her weight against the hydroplane control, notched it home, and dashed for the pumps, flogging at one for ten strokes and then at the other, then back to the first . . . she was gasping by the time she realized that Andy had stopped pumping and that day was now once again part of the light inside the hull.

"Missed it by feet," said Andy. "Where are we? Oh, I see, just off the point — not as far as I meant. Batteries getting low, maybe; or perhaps I got my sums wrong."

"What was it?" said Emma.

"The edge of the underwater cliff. We met it earlier than I expected because we came in off the point and not in the cove. It's all right, my lovey — I'd have let the safety weight go if I'd thought we couldn't clear it, and we'd have come up with a rush. But I didn't feel like wasting another day bashing pipes into shape. Care for some fresh air?"

"Yes, please."

"Me too. Mark you, it'll be worse than this by the time you've done a full trip with Ewan. Motor forward — half speed."

Emma wriggled back to her chair, pulled at the truncheon, saw the spark leap and heard the engine begin its slide up the scale. It never reached its proper note, though. Suddenly it hiccuped, jerked, tried again, juddered unrhythmically, shaking the whole hull.

"Motor off!" shouted Andy.

"What happened *this* time?" said Emma when the bronze cave was quiet again.

"Fouled the tail, I think. Now why — hey, how's your spirit level?"

Emma peered.

"We're a long way up at the tail, I think."

"Thought so," said Andy. "My fault. I knew you'd gone on pumping after I stopped. Never mind, we'll pump her up as far as she'll go and then we'll nip out and see what the damage is."

So there was more shoving levers to and fro, and by the time it was over Emma was really aware of how nasty the air was becoming — far worse than the air in a small classroom at the end of a long exam. She wondered how long it would take for the crew to breathe away so much oxygen that they would stifle. Two hours? Three? If they sat very still and didn't panic . . .

"That'll do," said Andy. "If they saw us surface they'll be up here in a few minutes and tow us ashore."

He sounded very calm after this final accident, as if he were determined to show Emma that he didn't always lose his temper when he was thwarted — after all, it had been at least half her fault — *she* ought to have checked the level before she started the motor . . . The hatch clicked and she heard the light scraping of the monster's nose settling forward against the hull, moving all in one piece with the hatch cover. Andy's legs were already flicking themselves neatly out of the hole; far more clumsily Emma followed him out into the delicious air.

Anadyomene lay just around the point where the young pines swooped down the hill. Emma could see most of the way down the loch, but not the actual shore where The Huts and the boathouses stood. If they had got a little further in they would have been completely hidden, which was all part of the plan. There were two problems: first to get the crew ashore unseen by the telly folk; second to hide *Anadyomene,* and this cove would do for both. The telly folk and their cameras would see the monster for the first and only time; then *Anadyomene* would come here, under the water, and surface out of sight; Ewan would unbolt the steel hoop that held the neck to the hatch in the thickness of the fiber glass; there would be a dinghy and a larger row-boat moored to a little buoy; in the large boat would be ballast weights — sacks of lead from Big House — which Ewan would lower into *Anadyomene* until the conning tower was half submerged; they would then shut the hatch, moor the bigger boat to the conning tower, pick up the little buoy and the head and row ashore in the dinghy.

113

They would hide the head in the wood. To anyone ashore it would look as though all the bay contained was a large rowboat moored to a greenish-colored buoy.

Andy was undressing, tossing his clothes back down the hatch. Emma sat on the rim of it and looked at the hill. After the stink and fright of the voyage she felt that the whole valley had been made all new for her, every pine needle, every pebble, every feather. The clean, almost surgical smell of the pines added to the newness and freshness. She felt the hull bobble and quiver as Andy slid down the side and swam round to the propeller; his head disappeared under the water for a few seconds, and then bobbed up again.

"It's a right old mess," he said. "Nip down and flood the forward tanks a little — that'll bring the screw up to where I can get at it. Not too much, or you'll go under; you'd better shut the hatch in case something goes haywire."

It was dreadful to go down alone, and prison yourself in, and turn the taps and listen to the water gurgle back, pulling the hull down. She let it happen in three-second bursts, with five seconds in between, until a double thump on the hull told her to stop. The tilt of the deck was quite marked as she climbed back and let herself out, to see Finn and Roddy rowing round the point.

"I've got all that," said Finn. "What's up? The beast looked marvelous through the view-finder, but you surfaced much too early when you got up here."

Andy explained what had happened. Roddy listened with an expression that made even Emma want to throw things at him.

"It doesn't sound too bad," said Finn. "I'll go back and

make a start on this lot. If I get going now we might be able to have a look at it this evening."

"Right," said Andy between his teeth, and dived quite unnecessarily underwater so as not to have to look at Roddy's face any more.

For some reason that was the best piece of film Finn ever took, though Ewan and Emma did almost a dozen more runs, becoming more expert each time. Perhaps it was the very expertise which made the subsequent runs look too smooth and unreal, whereas the awkward plunging of that first run somehow made it look as though the creature were swimming with huge, invisible strokes. They watched the film after supper, Finn fussing at the projector, Andy lounging and scratching, Mary sitting bolt upright on a chair at the back of the room, Miss Newcombe also sitting bolt upright like a child at her first play, Roddy yawning. First, to focus the projector, Finn ran a different piece of film taken at a time when Andy had had several friends staying and they'd organized a midnight water joust, lit from the shore by Finn's floodlights. Miss Newcombe squealed with pleasure at every splash, and Roddy too began to whoop as the white bodies tumbled and the diamond drops rose like fireworks against the black water. During one sequence, when Finn had managed to get close to a bearded man as he fell and had taken his plunge slow motion, Emma glanced over her shoulder and was astonished to see that Mary was sitting stony-faced. She was not normally a humorless or disapproving person.

Then there was darkness, mutterings from Finn, a square of blinding light on the screen, more mutterings, and a sort of foggy pattern. Finn fiddled with the projector and the fog became the lake — just dull gray with dull gray shore in the foreground, drab and amateurish. Nothing happened for a bit. Emma didn't even notice the first signs until they'd run the film through twice — a tiny blackness near the edge of the picture; then the head was well clear of the surface, the water rumpling behind it. The camera jerked and steadied and the head was now in the middle of the picture, not quite in focus, still coming up, the short curve of the neck going down to a wideness that might have been shoulders. The blurs sharpened and it was a beast from the deeps, tiny-headed, swimming purposefully with a slow dipping motion that suggested somehow the surge of large limbs beneath. The camera wavered, lost the beast completely, came back, and now you could see a curious disturbance some way behind the head, a dark curve that showed and vanished like the back of a dolphin, then came up in a different place, but smaller. The camera centered on the head again, wavered and came back. The beast, which had begun by swimming across the picture had wheeled slowly round and was now swimming almost away from the watchers, with the hummocks of its tail showing very clearly; and now it began to sink, still surging strongly forward. In half a minute it was gone and the lake was still. The film chattered for another minute, wildly searching the surface; then it fizzed and the screen was a white glare.

Roddy and Andy and Emma were all cheering and shouting. Emma saw Roddy stop, as though he'd only just remembered that he'd refused to have anything to do with the beast; Miss Newcombe was looking troubled.

"Well done, Finn!" said Andy. "Well done everybody! That's great!"

"Is that one of your jokes?" said Miss Newcombe. "I mean, it looked just as if there was something horrible in our loch."

"It's all right," said Andy gently. "It was only *Anadyomene* with a head stuck on. It's quite safe to swim still. But Poop, I want you to promise not to tell anyone what we've been doing. Promise?"

"I promise. I *thought* it was only what you've all been up to, but it looked so real, didn't it, Mary?"

"Indeed it did, Miss Poop. Though it did not look very like what my grandmother was telling me."

Before Emma had time to be startled by the matter-of-fact words, Finn laughed.

"You'll have to rethink what your grandmother told you," she said. "In fact we'd better get everyone together and coach them a bit, so they all tell something like the same story to the telly folk. We want to show these lowlanders they don't know everything."

"And they need showing," said Mary.

So that was the section of film which had been sent off to Glasgow, with a covering letter from Andy. Emma had rescued the rough draft from the wastepaper basket, and clipped it into her diary:

Dear Alistair
Dear Mr. McTurdle,
 I don't know if you remember me, but we met at a party of Gabriella Smith's last autumn. I think the enclosed bit of film taken by my sister Finn Fiona might interest you. She was trying to photograph some divers grebes for my father, who is away. We have taken more film since then, but this is still the clearest bit.

There have always been stories that we had a monster something like this in our loch. We've now seen it three days running, and so have several other people.

The oldest inhabitants say that its coming means trouble for the Clan, and that it last appeared in 1917 and 1944, when the world was too busy to pay attention. My theory is that it comes up at twenty-seven-year intervals. Anyway they say it swims about like this once a day for ten days and fifteen days and then disappears, so if you are interested you will have to be quick.

If Gabriella's still working with you, she knows the way here and we'd be glad to put you up. There's plenty of room.

If you aren't interested, would you please let me know at once, so that I can have a go at the BBC people.

Yours sincerely,
Andrew McAndrew
P.S. Love to Gabriella.

"That bit about the BBC will fetch them," said Andy. "They'll think I'm such a country cousin that I don't know how much they hate each other. Gabby'll ring up in three days to make sure we're not pulling their leg, and they'll come a couple of days later."

"Is Mr. McTurdle Gabriella's boss?" Emma had asked.

"Not exactly," Finn had said. "He's the personality, and

he knows it; he weighs about twenty stone but he's got a mean little voice however much he crinkles his eyes at the camera. They send him out on stunts like this, and he makes jolly jokes about being fat and asks mean questions between whiles. He usually works with a producer called Ken Gritt, and Gabriella's Mr. Gritt's assistant. She says he's nice and quiet and his real name's the Honorable Kenneth Grant."

In fact, they rang two days after the film was posted. You couldn't hear the telephone from the sitting room (a typical McAndrew arrangement) so it was Caitlin who came to tell Andy he was wanted from Glasgow. He was away several minutes and returned grinning with happy spite.

"That was Gabby," he said. "She told the others it was a leg-pull, but they think we couldn't have faked it. She sounded pretty miffed. They're coming tomorrow."

6

"I haven't written anything for three days,"
wrote Emma. "I was too tired the first day and
too ill after that." She looked out to where the
fine drizzle dimmed and unfocused land and
water. It was like being in the inside of a cloud.
The light all came from nowhere in particular,
so that the surface of the loch, pocked by innu-
merable tiny droplets, seemed to have no depth
beneath it. But there lay Anadyomene. . . . *And*
there . . . It was difficult to know where to be-
gin.

It began with being shaken awake. At one moment
Mummy was walking in through the door of their house in
Gaberones holding a huge bunch of sore-eye lilies — the

big red powder puff that springs up in the veldt, whose bulb is deadly poison and whose pollen can blind you — and Emma was trying to shout to her to drop them and wash her hands before she touched anything but the words wouldn't come; the next moment she was in a blur of darkness, still full of the panic of nightmare, being shaken.

Only it wasn't quite dark and she was lying in her bed in The Huts, sure that she hadn't had enough sleep. Roddy had stopped shaking her and was standing by her bed with his finger to his lips. He was fully dressed. The light must be the last remains of yesterday and not the beginning of tomorrow: Emma could believe in Roddy *staying* up, but not in his *getting* up.

"Go away," she said crossly. "I was having a dream."

"I need your help," said Roddy. "Please."

"Is something wrong? Are you ill?"

"No. I want you to help me about Andy. I've got a plan."

"Go away. I'm neutral. The whole thing's too stupid for words, besides spoiling my holidays."

"It's *his* fault."

"It's just as much yours. If you stopped needling him —"

"Look. Just this once, and that's the last time. I'll declare peace, unless Andy starts it up again. I promise."

"You're still being stupid. Of course Andy will start it up again. It'll be his turn."

"But he won't know. That's the whole point. I'll know, but he won't."

Drowsily, Emma struggled up until she could sit with her knees under her chin. She didn't often dream about Mummy; but if she went asleep again she'd find herself in some other dream, and anyway it had been a nightmare. She still felt furious with Roddy, but he looked so serious, so much as though he'd managed to think of *the* right answer but nobody would believe him, that she felt a bit sympathetic with him too.

"What's your plan?" she said.

"I want to take Anna out."

"Now! In the dark?"

"Yes."

"Can't you wait till morning? It's light by three, and —"

"There wouldn't be time to charge the batteries again. We're bound to run them down a bit, and if they went flat when the telly folk are filming, that'd spoil everything. I saw Andy go out and turn the generator off half an hour ago, but they're still all connected up. I know how to start it, and I can nip out in the early morning and turn it off again."

"Someone will hear it."

"Andy won't. He sleeps like a log. And anyone else will think it's him fiddling about."

"But Anna in the dark . . . anyway, what good would it do?"

"He never let me touch her. He treated me like an idiot, just there to waggle a few levers. And in that voice! I want to know I can."

"What'll you do? If I came, I mean."

"Drive her out into the middle of the loch. Do one dive —"

"No!"

"One short dive in the middle of the loch. One minute. There's nothing there to hit. Then come home."

"But it's dark. I mean it will be soon. It'll be terribly

dangerous, even like that. Anna isn't a toy, Roddy . . . it's a . . . I don't know, when I'm in it I think it's a *trap,* waiting to get one of us. I hate it."

"You didn't have to — oh, yes, I suppose you did. All right, Cousin Emma, I'll try to think of something else."

He sounded as he turned for the door as if all the rest of his life had gone sour — day after sour day. Emma knew that whatever his *something else* was it wouldn't be likely to be a declaration of peace. She was sick of the whole feud. It wasn't like ordinary quarrels in a family — the McAndrews played to hurt. And now it would be worse; so bad, perhaps, that despite Finn and Miss Newcombe and the heavenly valley she wouldn't be able to stand it any more; she'd pack and say good-bye and go back to the seething trailer camp in Dorset, where Uncle Dick didn't really want her . . .

"Roddy?"

He took his hand off the door handle.

"Yes."

"I'll come if you promise me two things."

"Yes?"

"We won't leave the jetty till it's really dark, and then we'll see how dark it is. If there's enough moon to see a bit ahead, we'll go, but it there isn't we won't try. And when we go under, it'll be for only a minute, right out in the middle — and only just under, too. That's the first thing."

"OK. That's what I was going to do anyway. There will be a quarter moon, too, I think."

"The other thing is that you really will call off the feud."

"I've said I will."

"I mean, even if he doesn't stop at once, you won't try to get back at him again."

"But . . ."

"I'll try and find a way of asking him to stop too. But if these TV people come and the plot works I think he will stop, provided you don't needle him. It's more your fault than his, it really is. You make him lose his temper just to show you can, and . . ."

Roddy laughed.

"OK," he said. "I'll try and break the habit. It is a habit, you know; rather like picking a scab. I'll wait for you on the verandah — climb out through your window when you're dressed."

It didn't take long, as she'd got the clothes she was going to wear the next morning ready before she got into bed. But she got an extra jersey out of the bottom drawer and put that on too.

As they were tiptoeing along the road in the pine-smelling night, one of the wildcats miaowed far out across the loch, and the echo answered it. It was now truly night, with a crooked moon slant in the sky behind them and the pattern of stars ahead blanking off where the mountainous horizon stood blacker than the darkness. Yes, thought Emma, if no clouds came up there would be light enough to see. She felt that what she was doing was foolish but inevitable: if she ever had to explain it, Daddy would never understand, though Mummy might. Again a wildcat called, the water making it sound surprisingly close, but as they were out of the line of the echo the sound only came once.

Emma frowned. The time before she had simply accepted the second noise as an echo, but really it must have been another cat, unless it was actually swimming in the loch. She must be still half asleep — dangerous for a night excursion in an eighty-year-old submarine.

"Shall we take the tail?" said Roddy, standing on the jetty and looking at the wicked fiber-glass head that jutted up from the bulge of metal.

"We'll have to. You can't take it off without swimming, and —"

"No. Andy fixed it after you tangled the propeller. There's a shackle a couple of feet along the line. I can hook it out with the boat hook."

"Well, if we did get into trouble it would be nice to be able to reverse, which you can't with the tail there."

"OK, hold the torch. Push the switch to the right when I tell you, not to the left, and shine it down."

"He handed her a big electric torch, the sort with a reflector in its side and a dome on the top, so that you can choose between seeing a long way in front of you or a short way all around. She put her foot on the ladder to steady it as he scuttled across, eased the beast forward onto its nose, and disappeared down the hatch. In a few seconds he came back, carrying a sort of stick; Emma switched the beam of the torch on and shone it down the hull, using her body to screen it from The Huts. When she had finished blinking at the light, bright as sunrise for the moment to her night-accustomed eyes, she saw that he was crouching on the slope of the hull and fishing for the tail with one of the stubby boat hooks. Emma steadied the ladder again as he crawled back with the tail cord between his teeth. He tied it to a pier of the jetty.

"Now I'll disconnect the leads."

Emma coiled the cables as he fed them up through the

hatch. Two minutes later she was sitting in the familiar chair; apart from the dregs of her drowsiness it might have been bright day outside. The hatch clanked shut above her.

"All right if I put the lights out?" said Roddy.

"I won't be able to see the level."

"You won't need to while we're on the surface. When we dive you can use the torch."

"Ready?" said Roddy and switched the lights off. "Motor forward."

"Are your eyes used to the dark already?"

He laughed. Mad though the enterprise was, it was pleasant to hear him so happy.

"All right, Cousin Cautious, I'll give them thirty seconds. . . . Ready? Motor forward."

In the true dark the spark across the motor switch leaped blindingly, and the hum rose along a slightly different curve from the one Emma was used to — probably because they weren't towing the tail. The light ripples tinkled against the bronze. She felt it would have been a blissful night to go for a sail or a row, to watch the big outlines of the hills and smell the night air; instead of which she was back in this metal bubble, which smelled of nothing but engine oil and rubber and vinegar.

"How much can you see?" said Emma.

"Different shades of black. I can see quite a stretch of water in front, so you needn't worry about our hitting anything, but all the shore's the same sort of color and Finn's cut the hole in the neck too low for me to see the skyline. Hang on a minute and we'll turn west. Now."

Emma felt the hull tilt to the slow curve.

"There," said Roddy, "I can see the sky at the end of the loch now. Not bad."

"How are we going to get back to the jetty?"

"We may have to open the hatch once or twice and poke our noses out. Don't forget I know this loch pretty well."

"And you've sailed on it at night?"

"As a matter of fact, no. It's against the rules."

"I hadn't realized there *were* any rules."

"Oh, yes. Mary makes them, and Father gives his assent. Like Parliament and the Queen. After that they're rules, and we don't break them."

"I'd have thought you were breaking that one now."

"Oh, this is different. It's a rule about *sailing*. Ready for a turn to port — we'll have to put the lights on to submerge, and I'd like the window to be facing away from The Huts, just in case anyone's awake. . . . That'll do. Motor off. Right, let's drift for a bit."

Emma listened to the diminishing noise of the ripples on the hull; they took a long time to reach stillness.

"Hey!" said Roddy, "What was that? Duck or something scuttling across in front of us. We must have given it a scare. Right, lights on. You'd better give the orders for submerging — you've had more practice than me."

Emma followed the familiar routine and listened to the familiar gurgles below deck. This was the bit that always made her palms sweat, which in turn made the stopcocks slippery to twist. They got the trim right, with the submarine barely buoyant, at the third adjustment; then Emma switched on the big lantern as Roddy switched off the lights. As usual — it was almost a superstition now — she checked the position of the weight release.

"Ready?" said Roddy. "Motor — Hey! *That's* not a duck!"

"What isn't? I wouldn't have thought you could see any-thing."

"Not much, but the surface is whitish from underneath, like a mirror, and there was something going across it, bigger than a dogfish."

"It might be one of Andy's pieces of rotting weed."

"Jet-propelled weed. It was going like a speedboat. There's another!"

"Let's follow them and see."

"Not a hope. They were going at least twenty knots. But they came from the same direction, and if we go that way . . . Motor on. What was that?"

"The spark," said Emma. "You always get one."

"No. Something hit the boat, just to the right of me. Didn't you feel it?"

"*Feel* it? Roddy, pay attention to the steering — you're all over the place — I can't keep level if . . . That's better. Roddy, we must have hit something. Do let's go up."

Emma cut the motor without orders, panicky. They were well underwater, as Roddy's inattention had sent them into a sudden dive, so there was not even the sound of a ripple to hide the slapping and grating jar of something biffing heavily into the metal just behind the conning tower — *behind,* so there was no question of *Anadyomene* having knocked against a submerged lot or something.

"Come around here, quick!" hissed Roddy. "Turn the torch off."

Emma banged her shin on the frame that held the bat-teries as she stumbled her way around in the blackness; she found Roddy by touch, and squeezed beside him into the broad seat. At once she saw something weird, but not at all like what Roddy had been talking about — short, green vertical lines poised in the corner of the window, and glowing. No, that was only the compass. The difficulty was to look through the glass and not just *at* it. Outside was emptier than anything she could imagine, no shape, no color, no depth, no distance.

"Wait," breathed Roddy. "I think we're going up, but only just. Wait. There!"

It was a hurtling shadow, going from right to left, long and thin at either end, with a bulge in the middle. It was impossible to guess whether it was a small shadow near or a huge shadow far, because there was nothing to measure distance by. Then another. Then . . .

This shadow, larger (perhaps it was nearer), turned from its path, towards the watchers. In the instant that its shape blanked out the whole window they heard the slapping grate and felt the hull jar.

"It attacked us," said Roddy. He sounded frightened, but interested — fascinated, even. Emma felt the same — she was chilly and trembling and couldn't stop swallowing at nothing, but also she wanted to *know*. More than all the terror she wanted to know.

"That light right up in the bows," she said, "does it turn on? I don't know if Andy fixed it, but it's there."

"Look," said Roddy, "there's one going the other way. Shut your eyes while I turn the lights on and look for the switch; then you won't have to get used to the dark again."

Emma pressed her palms against her eyelids and looked at the other dark, mottled with the drifting pattern of her own blood vessels.

"That one's the inside lights," she heard Roddy say. "Yes, I don't see . . . Oh, hang on a sec and shift forward a bit, it might be your side. Yes, that's it. Wow, it's a sort of searchlight. Shall I leave it on?"

With an effort Emma didn't look, but continued to stare into her private dark.

"Switch it off," she said, "and wait. Then we'll switch on the moment we see anything. That's how Daddy takes his animal photographs in the game reserves."

"You know best. OK, you can open your eyes. Feel along my arm and you'll find the switch — it goes sideways, forward, to go on."

Staring through the glass Emma began to feel along the rough jersey. Another shadow blinked in the slot of dark before she reached his fingers; it wasn't a switch — more like a little lever: if the light at the front really was a searchlight, perhaps it needed a more powerful current than an ordinary switch could cope with. Roddy edged back, and she felt his cheekbone hard against hers as he joined her in peering at the void.

"Can't see a thing," he grumbled.

"Wait."

"There!"

Emma flicked the switch and the darkness was water, green, glowing from underneath, and a shape was hurtling out of the orb of light, a gray blink now, solid and not a shadow, going so fast that tiny bubbles trailed behind it, glistening like dewdrops.

"Missed it," said Roddy, letting his breath go with a snort. "The tail's something like an eel. Switch off."

"I thought you said it was a searchlight," said Emma.

"It's a damn powerful light to show that much under-water," said Roddy. "Sit still. There!"

They missed the next one completely, and the third almost completely. They would have missed the fourth if it hadn't been two, coming from opposite directions half a second apart, so that while the one that came from their right was whisking out of sight, the one from their left was coming into their little slit of vision, too fast to stop. Although it was going like a torpedo it jerked itself sideways in the water almost at a right angle, lithe in its element as a swift is in the summer air. For an instant it was swimming straight at the conning tower, then with another flick it was out of sight, rocking the hull with the disturbance of its going.

Without thinking, Emma switched the light off, as though the show were over, then shut her own eyes to give her brain a chance to sort out and tidy the mess of images that her retina had gathered.

Flippers like a turtle's but no shell, a thin, lashing tail, a body about as big as a sack of corn, but shaped and curved to slide through the water, and of a gray, dead, fungussy color as though the sun had never shone on it; the neck had been already curving towards her as her eyes unblinked from the shock of light, so that she hadn't seen how long it was — but long, long; and a lizard head, earless, tiny-eyed, huge-mouthed — a lizard mouth running back along the skull, lipless, so that all the ragged teeth showed. Out of the corner of this mouth hung the tails of two fishes.

"There's never *been* anything like that," whispered Roddy.

"Yes there has. Finn did some drawings when she was choosing a shape for our beast. She got them out of a book, the one she was reading in your boat that first day."

"It's not a dinosaur. Dinosaurs were monsters. Huge."

"Mary never talks about monsters. She calls it 'the creature.' "

"There's one, and —"

Emma found she still had her eyes shut, was still seeing those teeth, that head. As she opened them to take an interest once more, she heard a new noise, a gentle watery sound. The world outside the window had a roof now, a roof of wavering silver, which was suddenly rumpled as one of the black shadows, headless, hurtled across it.

"We've surfaced," said Roddy. "What shall we do?"

"Let's get the window above water and see where we are."

"OK. I'll put the lights on."

The steady efficiency of the pumps was calming. When Emma settled back to her seat she found that in spite of the exercise her heart was now beating at something like its proper rate. But Roddy had hardly turned the lights out when the hull shook again to the slap and grate of another onslaught. She knew what it was now.

"They're trying to take a bite out of Anna," she said.

"Then they got sore teeth," said Roddy. "They must be pretty stupid; Anna doesn't look anything like a fish."

"I don't think they can see anything. They're night animals, but if they used their eyes they'd be huge, like owls'. I think they hunt by smell — they've only attacked the places where we've stood, and mostly we've had bare feet."

"D'you remember Mary's story about the poachers when Andy was two? They came at night and two of their boats were upset and three men vanished. Eaten, I bet."

He sounded pleased about it, but Emma felt sick.

"Where are we?" she said.

"I can't see a thing. Just water and dark. We'll have to do a circle and I'll try and spot the end of the loch. Ready?"

Just outside the conning tower, incredibly close, a wild-cat miaowed.

"No!" shouted Emma. "We must be right up against the shore. Didn't you hear that cat?"

"That was no cat," said Roddy. "That was one of the creatures — they call like that, I bet. No wonder I've never been able to find any wildcats. It's OK, Cousin Emma, I can see yards of water. Motor on."

The blue spark dazzled the dark, and the motor's hum rose, strangely comforting. Emma felt the hull tilt as Roddy took *Anadyomene* in a tight curve.

"There it is," he said. "Hang on, I'm still going round . . . and there's Deil's Cleugh — I can see the waterfall. Motor off. So . . . we must be pretty well bang in the middle of the loch, but quite a long way up it, east of The Huts, I mean, up towards the shallow end. What do you fancy?"

"Go home and tell the others. You've got the TV people coming. You've got to decide what to do."

"Andy won't believe us. He'll think it's part of what you call the feud."

"If I tell him."

"You don't know how obstinate he is. Cousin Emma?"

"Yes."

"One of them had a fish in its mouth."

"Yes."

"They've all been going the same way as that one, or exactly the opposite way. And there aren't any fish down here."

"Oh, I see. You mean we've been on the path up to the

shallow end, where the fish are, and that one was taking fish back to where they live — to feed its young, or something. Where *do* they live?"

"*I* don't know. Did you see any gills?"

"No. And the dinosaurs breathed air. And a lot of them swim with their heads out of the water. Oh, there's so much to find out! We've *got* to stop the TV people coming."

"No hope of that now. It's all settled, and anyway it makes the whole thing much more interesting. Hoards of tourists, and —"

Roddy, they've got through sixty million years by the skin of their teeth . . ."

"Sore teeth now."

"Oh, shut up! It's the loch, it must have something very peculiar about it which let them get through the Ice Ages and go on hunting and breeding. It's a balance, and they've adapted to it. There've never been enough McAndrews round the loch to alter the chemistry of the water; you haven't got enough farmland for the fertilizer to make a difference, and the same with sewage and things. But tourists will change all that — tourists will kill them. On my uncle's farm —"

"Unless they kill the tourists," said Roddy with a laugh. "They'll want to go night-bathing — we'll have to get Old Crow to insure against people being eaten. I say, I wonder how much Mary knows — she always hated us swimming even by daylight — that's why none of us are much good — and the night Finn took that film, the one you saw, she practically threw a fit."

"Perhaps the creatures are frightened of light. Finn had her floodlights on, didn't she? What are we going to *do?*"

"Find out where they come from, if we can. We'll track them along the surface. Are you game?"

"For a bit," said Emma.

The track to the hunting grounds was surprisingly narrow, and Roddy's circle to get his bearings had taken them away from it, so they quartered the loch in vain for ten minutes before Roddy gave a yelp of triumph. And now, for some reason, far fewer of the creatures were swimming on the surface, only the occasional head surging clear for a few yards — to breathe, Emma thought. They lost the track again, found it, lost it . . .

"It'll be easier underwater," said Roddy. "Provided they're still swimming at all."

So once more they submerged and began their search below the surface. The difficulty now was that with *Anadyomene* uncontrollable at speeds below one knot they had to do their tracking in sudden rushes and stops. Sitting by the motor lever, listening to the hum of the motor and Roddy's grunts and ejaculations, all Emma's old fears returned. She could see nothing except the jigging bubble in the tube; she could do nothing except obey orders; she could only endure. She tried to think about all the brave men who had chosen, during wars, to lurk underwater in similar metal traps while their enemies tried to guess where they were and drop the ripping explosives down on them. They must have been even more afraid, and yet they had chosen to do it again and again. The thought of the depth charges led Emma to think about *her* enemies in the water, and to realize that she was not so afraid of them as she was of the water itself. M. Goubet's good bronze would keep *them* out — unless they were to track *Anadyomene* home to the jetty, lured by the meat smell; their necks were certainly long enough to reach up, and . . . It was curious that they hadn't attacked the fiber-glass head. Perhaps the smell of the resin . . .

"On course now," said Roddy suddenly. "We can speed up a bit. There's a big 'un. Just about as many coming as going — I suppose they've got to get a lot of hunting in. This time of year there's only four hours of real dark. About Mary, Cousin Emma — I don't think she *knows* anything. Not what you and I would call knowing. It's more of a very strong superstition. I mean, it's *unlucky* to swim in the dark, all the McAndrews think that. I know Father made Poop promise not to, because it would offend Mary and the others. But Andy's friends didn't mind offending people, of course."

"It would probably only be unlucky if you went swimming up in the hunting grounds, or on their track to and fro," said Emma.

"Damn, I've lost them. Stand by for a turn."

"Where are we?" Emma's voice was sharp with panic, but she didn't mind. The hull was already beginning to tilt to the right.

"Running down the far side of the loch, I'm pretty certain. I've been keeping an eye on Andy's compass. Not far from the cliffs, I shouldn't be surprised, so I'm turning away from them. It's all right, Cousin Emma. You're in safe hands."

"Oughtn't we to surface?"

"It takes such ages. Halfway around now — should pick them up soon. . . . Yes, there goes one. . . . Are we level?"

"Yes."

"It was diving, then. Slow your motor. Down we go."

"But Roddy —"

"Reverse motor! Not just stop. Reverse!"

"I can't. I've got to wait for it to stop or I'll burn it out!"

"Oh, damn! Oh damn!"

"What's happening? There, it's stopped."

Emma slammed the lever into full-speed reverse, and listened to the motor's rising growl, deeper than usual because of the extra strain of taking way off the boat.

"I'm turning the outside light on," said Roddy in a quivering voice. "Wow, we're — motor off!"

But he didn't need to say it, because above their heads came a rasping noise that shook the hull like a drum — not enough to jar them in their seats but enough to make the bronze bubble vibrate with a bass groan. The engine too, before Emma snatched her hands off the weight release and pulled the lever into neutral, groaned deeper and deeper as it slowed, shoving against something too solid to move.

"Caught the fiber-glass head on something," said Roddy, breaking the sweaty silence.

"Where are we? What's happened?"

"I can't see much, but we're under some sort of rock. I can just see the edge of it."

"The edge of it *ahead* of us?"

"Yes."

More silence, during which Emma could hear the faint scrape of the fiber glass nudging against whatever it had touched, held there by *Anadyomene*'s slight buoyancy.

"If we flood the tanks a bit we'll begin to sink," said Roddy. "That might clear the head enough for us to reverse out."

"All right."

Emma could hardly whisper. To be actually sinking . . . But hardly had the gurgling stopped when they heard the gentle rasp of the keel settling onto rock.

"We'd better try it like that, even so," said Roddy in a firmer voice. Emma couldn't speak, but settled back in her seat.

"Ready?" said Roddy. "Half speed reverse."

The motor hum rose, reached a peak, dipped, growled.

"Motor off," said Roddy, and rattled on as though he were afraid of letting the silence settle again. "I didn't hear the keel move, but it's lead and we might not. If we made a bit back then, we may have cleared the head from whatever was touching it, and — hello, there's one. It popped down beyond the end of the rock as though it was coming out, and then it saw us and popped straight back again. Let's pump her buoyant and try again."

It was no good.

"We got *in,* damn it!" said Roddy angrily. "Let's . . ."

But that was no good either. Nor was the next try. Nor the next.

"We're in some sort of tunnel," said Roddy, ten minutes later. "I wonder if I put the propeller right over to one side — we might be able to swing her slowly round and then we could see our way out."

"No!" said Emma. "You'll get jammed across it, and then . . . Roddy?"

"Yes."

"Have you been listening to the motor?"

"What about it?"

"It's giving up quicker. As soon as we start pushing

against something it gives up. We're running out of electricity."

"Rot!"

"No."

"All right. I'd noticed too. You should see how the light dims when you're taking current. We must think of something else."

"Roddy, that creature you saw just now — did it look as if it was really going *up?*"

"Yes."

"How deep are we?"

"Shine the torch round . . . twelve feet."

"I'm sure they breathe air, and there's such a lot of them they must have a big space to live in. We're only twelve feet under, and the one you saw came down and went up. It might be just beyond that ledge: we'd have room to turn around and come out again forward . . . we could wait till it was light outside, too. There's bound to be a little light from outside."

Roddy thought about it.

"You want to go further *in?*" he said.

"Yes. It's the best chance. Besides . . . besides, if we're going to get stuck, don't let's get stuck here. If we go in, at least we'll find out. I want to *know* before I . . . before . . ."

Astonishingly, Roddy laughed.

"Don't say it," he said. "I've never heard a madder reason."

"It's not as mad as Finn getting drowned rather than marry Andy Fertagh," said Emma sourly.

He laughed again.

"OK," he said. "We'll just give the batteries a rest. Sometimes they pick up a bit when you do that. I'll turn the light off, too."

Almost at once the hull was shaking to the steady onslaught of the creatures. For a moment Emma thought that they were actually going to do the trick of bundling *Anadyomene* bodily out into the open loch, but then she heard through the racket the grinding of the fiber-glass head against the tunnel roof.

"I can't stand *this*," shouted Roddy. "Light on! There they go! You're right — they really hate it. Motor on!"

Emma hauled at the lever. The motor ground sluggishly up the scale, and leveled off nowhere near its proper note.

"We're moving," said Roddy. "Come along, you poor old thing, come *along!* Keep going, just a bit more. Come along. Easy, easy. There. Motor off."

Even the blue spark was tired.

"Shine the torch round here," said Roddy. "Yes, we're going up. Oh, damn!"

Rock grated near the tail. Emma snatched the torch back and watched the bubble move forward as the bow rose while the tail stayed fast. Then there was a longer scraping, a twitch of the hull, a rattle from the propeller, and the bubble stayed where it was.

"Nothing much," said Roddy. "Slid out of it. I can see the surface now, at this tilt . . . wait for it . . . we're there."

Emma heard the rattle of water breaking from the fiber glass, and behind it a faint, wailing noise, like wind in a chimney.

"I'm going to switch the light off," said Roddy. "Then we'll pump her higher. If they attack us like they did in

140

the tunnel, we'll have to switch on again; but that may only have been because we were blocking the tunnel. I want to rest the batteries as much as possible. Lights off. I wonder what that noise was. It's stopped now."

7

*"The noise was the creatures, of course," wrote
Emma. "I think they make it when they see a
light, and even the wildcat noise is what they do
when they first come out of the cave and see the
moon. They hate light."*

*A movement caught her eye outside her win-
dow — the Jaguar hissing through the drizzle
with Poop bouncing in her seat beside Andy like
a child waiting for a circus to start.*

*"Light hurts them," wrote Emma. "You can
hear it in the noise they make. When Roddy
first poked the torch up through the hatch . . ."*

"They're leaving us alone, then," said Roddy after he
and Emma had sat waiting a couple of minutes for the on-

slaught. "They're learning. Shine the torch this way so that I can find my pumps. Fine. We'll pump her out as far as she'll go — I want to get that head off if I can."

"Why? How?"

"So it doesn't catch in the rock on the way out. We aren't going to have enough juice to allow for that. Ewan's left the right wrench here, ready for tomorrow."

"It's probably today by now."

"Half past twelve. You're right. Up we go."

As she worked the pumps Emma discovered how bad the air inside the hull had become. She pumped slowly, so as not to use up more oxygen than she had to, but Roddy's impatience made him flog the levers to and fro so that he finished long before her.

"That'll do," he said. "Let's see what happens if we raise the lid an inch and poke the torch up. You watch through the port."

He was already kneeling on the seat when Emma crept around and, crouching clear of him, cupped her hands on either side of her eyes like blinkers and pressed them against the glass.

"It's *warm!*" she said.

"So's the hatch."

"This is where the hot springs must be. This is how they got through the Ice Ages — in here! That's why they can't stand light! That's —"

"Hold it," snapped Roddy, cutting off her excited gabble. "Now's what matters. Turn, you brute."

Click, went the clasp, and light dazzled across the water. Slimed rock on the extreme right. A band of water, seen from only a couple of inches above the surface, rippling green and yellow in the yellow light. The clamor of the creatures racked her through and through — not a miaow, but an endless, wavering yell. One of the lizard heads plopped out of the water a few feet in front of the bows and coming towards her, but in an instant it was streaking away. Then the whole scene became a blaze of white foam as the hull rocked and plunged beneath a buffet from above, up near the bows. A few drops sprinkled the back of her neck. The yelling cut short, and she realized that Roddy had let the hatch fall, but he still had the torch on and in the thin beam that shone from either side of her cupped hands she saw one, two, three much smaller creatures slip into the water. One of them touched the hull, but she could only just sense the slight jar, as *Anadyomene* was still lurching from the original blow.

"Wow, what a stink!" said Roddy. "Did you see what hit us?"

"I think we've come up beside a rock, and a big one jumped off it to get away from the light. It must be used to the water being deep there — they wouldn't splash like that if they were diving normally. Three babies followed it. Are you all right?"

Roddy's face was very pale and he was gulping slightly.

"Think so. It's the stink. Didn't you smell it?"

"I smelled something pretty nasty, but the air's so bad down here anyway, and I was too busy looking to notice."

"It's like . . . like . . . I won't say it. But perhaps it's why they aren't chewing at us anymore. They make so much pong in here that they can't even notice our pong on the hull."

"What are we going to do?"

"They seem to be scared of the light all right. If we can put up with the stench we'll try and get the head off. I'll go the same way as last time, put the hatch up a little, give them plenty of time to clear off, and then climb out. When I'm out you'll have to follow me and hold the torch while I work. Here we go. Hold your nose."

This time, as the hatch rose, Emma saw two of the heads darting across her line of sight. The ragged teeth were made for tearing, not chewing. A little hump which might be nostrils rose at the top of the snout, near the front, like a crocodile's but flatter. The heads were the color of toadstools all over except for a black streak down the back of them. The eyes were even smaller than she'd thought, little black beads sewn onto the toadstool skin . . .

She felt a blow on her shoulder, and looked up. Roddy was kicking her, and she realized that she had become so absorbed in the effort to remember every detail of what she saw that she had never noticed that the clamor from the creatures was too loud to shout through. She climbed out of the hatch, into the reek.

The vast cave stank. It was all horrible things, everything slimy and rotten and hidden from the sun, but mostly fish. And all the time the long yelp beat at her brain.

Roddy handed her the lamp and pointed to where the fiber-glass head lay back along the hull. Gingerly, she balanced herself around on the curving metal above the stinking water and crouched to steady the head for him. The hull rocked at every move. Suddenly, terror of an attack from behind overcame her, and she twitched herself around, almost losing her foothold; rock soared there, only just aft of *Anadyomene*'s propeller, and arched over them before it was lost in darkness, and a rock ledge, against which the submarine nestled, ran out beside them and became the cave wall — no attack from that side, unless there were a creature still on the ledge. The hull joggled and she turned back; Roddy was lowering himself down the hatch.

He was gone for only a few seconds and came back with a coil of rope, one end of which he fastened to the shackle by the conning tower. He turned to her and she saw his lips form the words "hold tight"; the hull bucketed as he leaped for the slippery rock, scrabbled, and climbed to the ledge. She saw the cord tauten as he hauled the hull in close against the rock; then there was a long pause, with him out of sight, looking for a projection to tie it to, presumably. And then he was back, poised on the ledge.

He just stood there.

All around the high, wailing bellow continued, but nothing came into the circle of light. Emma thought how fast the creatures could move through the water, in how few seconds they would be on them if the torch went out, if she dropped it. The first thing was . . . no . . .

Holding the torch above her head she lowered herself into the hatch and felt for the boat hook, pulled it out of its catches and fed it up through the hatch beside her. Back again on deck she lifted the fiber-glass head and closed the hatch. That would give him something solid to jump against. He had the cord already. Now she reached out the boat hook to him.

He reached for it, felt for the cord, shut his eyes, opened them, stared at her and shook his head.

Well then, thought Emma, crosser than her fear, I'll have to lower him from above.

She hooked the lamp onto the boat hook and passed it up. Then she grasped the cord, leaped, and scrabbled.

Roddy had her by the back of her jersey and half pulled it over her head as he hauled her the last two feet.

"Sorry," he yelled. She smiled sourly.

When she'd settled her jersey and looked down, she at once understood and was sorry for the sourness. It might be only a few feet, but the green, wet metal of the submarine seemed a tiny and treacherous landing place in the dark water from which, even as she watched, another of the lizard heads shot up and shied away. She moved back and stepped into softness. A softness like a pile of rotten leaves. Roddy moved the torch.

She was standing on the edge of a nest, a two-yard circle of waterweed, slightly hollowed in the middle. On the edge of the circle of light, further along the ledge away from the cave entrance, she thought she could see the edge of another nest. Without thinking she flicked the switch in the side of the torch so that the light no longer shone out of the dome on top to make their protective circle round them, but shot in a long searchlight beam from the side. As she swiveled the beam down the cave wall the water exploded into a boiling flurry as creature after creature flung itself from the line of light into the water. In one place she saw a nest which seemed to be still palpitating, and then four or five little lizards, none of them a foot long, had not dived but tumbled over the edge. As she flicked the switch back to the less fierce illumination of the dome, Emma found herself hoping that the little nightmares could swim.

Roddy was tugging at her elbow, so she picked her way out of the odious softness of the nest. He pointed to the next ledge above them. Emma tried to mime surprise — it wasn't easy to be tactful when you couldn't even talk. He took the torch out of her hand and put it down against the rock, then screened it from the cave with his body. The yell of protest diminished to individual sharp yelps, backed by a continuous whimpering; but as that torture was taken away, Emma was again aware of the stench, borne on the steamy air of the hot springs. The sweat of terror was mixed with the sweat of heat and humidity; all her skin was streaming under her two jerseys.

"I can get down *there* again," said Roddy, pointing to the ledge. "I think I can get down to Anna if I *have* to. I don't know why I came up, except that I was frightened of being attacked from behind while I was dealing with the head and wanted to be sure we were moored close in. I don't think they can reach more than this ledge by the water — they can hardly move on land. They get up as far as this by throwing themselves out of the water, like dolphins. I could see what they were doing better when you were holding the torch. So if we can get up there we can have a bit of a rest."

Emma knew that she must rest. The next ledge was level with her head, and first of all she settled the lantern firmly onto it, as though that were more precious than either of them. The maddened and maddening wail began at once. Roddy gave her a leg up, and then she hauled him from above. This ledge was not level, but sloped up towards the heart of the hill, and Roddy pointed up it. Emma was sick with tiredness and fear and the stink and heat of the great cave. She longed to sink to her knees, cuddle herself close, and let the world go black. Roddy looked at her fiercely, took her by the wrist, and almost dragged her up the slope. A part of her mind noticed that they were now walking over a different kind of softness, like rotten leaves on the floor of a forest, a very old forest. She looked down and saw a fine gray powder, which their footsteps stirred. It was arranged in a jumble of patterned ridges, and these too were part of a larger pattern, big circles, ten feet across. So once there had been nests up here. The creatures had been more active, or the water level had been higher. She wondered how long ago. Before Columbus? Before the Conquest? Before Christ? Yes, all of those. Perhaps when the glaciers melted . . . How long ago was that? She would look it up when . . .

Not when, *if*.

Roddy was walking with the boat hook under his left arm and the torch in his left hand, close to the edge of the ledge. Although they had only climbed two ledges, they were now four levels up — all the ledges tilted like this one, then. The whole hill was tilted, and the layers of rock of which it was made ran up on parallel slopes. In her tiredness it was some time before she thought of slipping her hand out of Roddy's and taking the torch from him. He looked around as she put it in her right hand, furthest from the water, and walked on, holding it as low as possible.

The clamor faltered, died, welled out where the ledge narrowed and she had to let the creatures see the beam direct, and diminished again.

"Hang on a sec," said Roddy. "Let's have that torch."

She gave it to him where the ledge widened, and he turned and faced across the cave, grinning as the hideous baying rose. Suddenly he switched the light off. His voice, deep and pompous, filled the silence.

"Thank you, thank you, thank you," he said. "I cannot tell you how deeply I am affected by the welcome you have given me. My friends, fellow citizens, fellow *Scots* . . ."

The light flicked on and the mad mob bayed. This time he moved the torch slowly back and down so that the noise lessened bit by bit.

"Thank you again. It is a name of which we are all proud — all *justly* proud —"

They nearly lost the torch over the ledge as Emma snatched it from him and switched it off.

"But it's exactly like," he said. "You must have heard them on the telly."

Emma found herself choking in the dark, choking with rage and tiredness.

"It *hurts* them," she said, over and over again. "Can't you hear how it *hurts* them?"

"*Them?*" said Roddy in an astonished voice. "They're vermin. They're — oh, all right. I'm sorry. Let's sit here — I don't think anything can get at us here."

They eased themselves down in the dark. To Emma it seemed not quite so warm up here, and the appalling stench was certainly less, and best of all they had silence. No, not silence, for the water was in ceaseless turmoil thirty feet below them. Sometimes a single yelp rang back and forth, but mostly it was the swash and splash of water as the creatures dived and leaped, and a little shrilling cry which Emma thought might be the babies clamoring for food as a parent returned.

She fidgeted with her shoulder blades and found a place where the rock wall seemed to welcome her, and said, "I'm going to sleep."

"No you mustn't," said Roddy. "You'll be much worse when you wake up."

She propped her eyelids open with her fingertips, but even so images began to jostle and shift in her head and words and phrases to flutter in and out like nesting martins. Her lips moved.

"The dark abysm," she said. "This is the dark abysm."

"Whassay?" said Roddy, sounding just as sleepy.

"I said this was the dark abysm. And it is."

She was awake now. But into her relaxing mind had slid a whole jumble of ideas and pictures on which the two mysterious words had acted like words of power, ordering them all together into the one shape that made sense. As when God had spoken, in just such a dark as this, "Let there be light." And there was light.

"Listen," she said. "This is important. Your grandfather hated Darwin, but suddenly he built a cairn to him. He put it in the wrong place on the hill. Miss Newcombe smelled something up there. He built it the year after he built *Anadyomene,* which he built to explore the loch to see if there was a monster in it. He put a curse on it, against anyone moving it. You got halfway there with your joke about Mother Mulligatawny. When somebody builds a monument to somebody he hates and puts it in a place that doesn't look right, it's because he has something to hide underneath it. And listen, that bit of Shakespeare. In the dark backward and abysm of time. It makes sense about Darwin and evolution, but it makes much more sense if you know that this cave's here, with the creatures in it. It's a sort of joke, and what's more it's a typical McAndrew sort of joke, building a monument to a man you hate to hide something which you know about and he doesn't . . ."

"Darwin was dead by then," said Roddy.

"That wouldn't make any difference to the McAndrews — and putting that line on it, with two meanings . . ."

Roddy thought about it.

"You're a good guesser," he said at last. "I said so the first day I met you. You might be right. Poop did smell something — she's got sensitive nostrils, too. You think there's a way in up there and Grandfather blocked it off?"

"A way out," said Emma. "What's the time?"

"Quarter past one."

"We might try and find it for an hour. There's no point in going back to Anna before daylight. How long will this battery last?"

"It's almost new and it's supposed to do twelve hours."

"Then that's all right. Roddy?"

"Yes."

Emma hesitated, then spoke very quickly, to get it over.

"You've got to be sensible. You mustn't rush up anything you won't be able to get down. *I* can't carry you."

He laughed, felt for her, put his arm round her shoulders, and kissed her clumsily on the ear.

"I'll be as sensible as a . . . as a *Tupper,*" he said.

The hour was up. They were so far from the water that whichever way they shone the torch not a yelp protested. Emma's elbow was grazed from a fall down a sloping rock, and Roddy's face was white in the torchlight.

"No luck," he said. "It looks like you guessed wrong, for once."

"It's still the only thing that makes sense," said Emma.

They had found that the back of the cave was wedge-shaped, the floor and the tilted ledges rising to meet the roof. The meeting was not even, the point of the wedge didn't end all along the same line, but raggedly. This meant that among the huge boulders fallen from the roof there were openings that seemed to lead further into the hill. Most of them ended in a few yards, but three had seemed more promising; the first, though, had merely led them round to the far side of the cave and started down to the water; the second had gone uphill for another forty or fifty yards and been blocked not by rock but by a black and oozing mass.

"Peat hag," Roddy had said hopefully. "At least it means we're pretty near the surface."

"Couldn't we dig our way out?"

"With *this?*" he asked, brandishing the boat hook. "We'd probably just get a lot of stinking water pouring all over us. Some of these hags are forty or fifty feet deep. Back we go."

And now they were at the end of the third tunnel, which ended in a chasm; a crack in the rock, four feet across, and beyond it the blank rock of the hill.

"Let's have another rest, anyway," said Roddy. "Then we'll go back. It ought to be light in half an hour. Do you mind if I smoke?"

"Smoke? *Do* you?"

"It steadies the nerves, that's what they say. Let's experiment."

"Not me," said Emma quickly.

Roddy laughed.

"I've been nicking Andy's cheroots," he said. "He's try-

153

ing to cut down to five a day by putting only five into that little case each morning, but he's never quite sure when he's halfway through whether he's had two or three; so I try to catch him when he's had two and nick one then, and he thinks he's smoked it. I'm being very brotherly, really, cutting him down to four. But I suppose you'll want me to give it up, as part of the bargain."

"I don't know," said Emma, too tired to think about it.

His first match went out in the draft, but he shielded the second and puffed busily away. Emma sniffed at the sweet smoke streaming past her nose — usually she hated tobacco smoke of any kind, but although the stench of the creatures was far less up here in the tunnel, it was still nasty enough to make this treacle-and-bonfire odor bliss by comparison. It was going to be hell going down to the real stench again, and —

"Roddy!"

"All right. I'll put it out. It's rubbish about the nerves, but at least it didn't make me sick — sicker than I am already, I mean."

"No, don't."

She seized his wrist before he could stub the cheroot out on the rock.

"There was a draft," she gabbled. "It blew your match out. And look where the smoke's going!"

Roddy moved his hand to the edge of the crack, while Emma held the torch. She had to hold it at just the right angle for them to see the thin trail of smoke at all as it whirled away, down over the edge and sideways along the crevasse. She flicked the switch to the searchlight position and they lay on the edge of the crack and peered down. The rock walls narrowed towards each other, and became no more than a slit, six inches across, but they could see no bottom.

"Ugh!" said Roddy, shivering, and drew back. Emma stayed where she was and played the beam sideways in the direction in which the smoke had gone.

"Look along there, if you can bear it," she said, and he crawled back. To their right the walls of the crack shelved in more sharply under the tunnel wall, and where they touched there was a floor of sorts, fallen scree which had been unable to fall further, only about ten feet below the level at which they lay.

"If we could get down there . . ." said Emma.

"Not me," said Roddy.

She played the beam along the near wall of the crevasse. It had never weathered. She wondered if this was the place at which the two vast layers of rock had torn apart when the hill tilted, leaving the cave between. The surface was rough, with plenty of handholds.

"Let me go and explore," she said. "I'm sure I can climb down there. You wait here, and if I don't find anything soon I'll come back. We *must* be near the top, because of that peat hag."

"OK. I'll tie the torch onto the loop at the back of your trousers."

In fact it was harder than it looked, although Emma had spent most of her seaside holidays climbing along the cliffs at Plettenberg Bay, because she hadn't been allowed to swim. But now there was no strength in her arms, hands and fingers; even a simple grip was exhausting and began to slip from her grasp before she was ready for the next move. Suddenly, when she was halfway down, her fingers failed her altogether, although her foot was firm in a crack. With a gasping grunt she reeled outward from the rock, something caught her a huge blow between the shoulder blades and a sharp and painful jab further down her spine. Almost she allowed her legs to crumple, but she kept them stiff and hung there, wedged between wall and wall, while the glass of the torch tinkled below her in the dark.

"Not too good," said Roddy's voice above her. "Are you all right?"

"I think so. I think I can work along to the passage like this. I don't think I can come up."

"What about the torch? Try using the other switch if you can reach it."

She fumbled round behind her and clicked the little piece of metal over. No light came.

"Not too good," said Roddy again. "What now?"

"I'll have to go on. I might be able to get out and go and get help. I didn't have far to go when I fell."

"It won't do," said Roddy. "There's nothing to tell you that the crack doesn't widen out again. You might simply fall down."

"If I had something to prod with. Can you try and reach me the boat hook?"

"Hang on, I'll lean over and swing it your way. It might just reach. Talk, Emma, so I can guess where you are."

"Make me a willow cabin at your gate," said Emma, "and call upon my soul within the house, write loyal cantons of condemned love and sing them loud even — that's it, that's my ankle, you've lost it, yes there. Hold it there and I'll see if I can reach it. . . . No, if I lean any more forward I'll fall. Work it out, away from the wall, along my leg, if you can. Got it!"

"Wow," said Roddy above her. "My wrist wouldn't have

156

stood much more of that. Cousin Emma, I've still got some matches."

"Keep them for the minute. I think I'm all right. We might need them if we've got to go back."

Roddy snorted.

"We can't go back," he said. "Without the torch the creatures would get us in five seconds flat."

As if to agree with him, a far yelp echoed up through the tunnels.

Knowing there was nothing else for it, Emma eased to her right. The boat hook was a nuisance until she hooked it into her belt, and the torch clattered behind her every time she shifted her back. She guessed each move was two inches, about, so she counted up to thirty of them before she rested, unhooked the boat hook, and waved it vaguely to her right. At once it rapped into stone. Prodding below her she found stone again.

"I'm there," she said.

"Take it easy," said Roddy. "You don't know whether any of that will bear you."

Gingerly she worked herself down, felt with a toe, eased her weight over, and stood. Prodding with the hook and waving her free hand before her face she crept shrinkingly forward. The floor was as uneven as the bed of a stream. Each step took several seconds. After a few minutes she was overpowered by the loneliness and dark, and called aloud, wordlessly.

"All right?" said Roddy's voice, echoing and distant behind her.

"Yes," she called, "so far. It's quite firm."

Her ears were singing, and her eyes seemed to have a gray film in front of them. A rock tilted under her feet and flung her off balance. She dropped the hook and flung out her hand to steady herself against the wall, then straightened and stood reeling. It was several seconds before she understood what her body had understood already, that her hand had known where it would find the wall. That the gray film was light.

Not daylight, but the light that prisoners see between the bars of their cells when the sunlit streets and squares are along two corridors and up a flight of steps. If she hadn't been so long in the dark her eyes would never have been able to see that it was light at all. She called the news to Roddy, picked up the boat hook, and stumbled on.

It took about forty yards to bring her to a place where the crack began to close to a narrowness that would not let her through, and here she stopped and looked up. The light was still faint, about thirty feet above her, but strong enough now to see that it filtered in in several places up there, and that the crevasse stretched right up to it. She let out a long breath and, now feeling immeasurably stronger, felt her way back towards Roddy.

It meant going into total blackness, prodding again and stumbling, and falling twice.

"Talk to me," she called. "Where are you?"

"Here," came the echoing voice. "I'll tell you the story of my life, shall I? And how I got into these evil ways. It's a sad story."

"A sad, sad, story," said Emma automatically. The words took time to reach him, and he had already begun to talk again, but he stopped and laughed before telling her about the miserable little house in Bootle where he'd been brought up by a sailor uncle who used to beat him with his wooden leg. Emma stumbled towards the stream of non-sense thinking about her cousin and wondering whether this was his way of nerving himself for what he was going to have to do. That climb, for Roddy, was going to be worse than anything Emma could think of, worse even than if she'd been told to pick up a poisonous snake . . .

"Can you strike a match?" she said at last. "I think I might be near the edge. I've had an idea."

"So've I," said Roddy.

The spark of light flared, dimmed, and then surprisingly transformed itself into a dark yellow light, with smoke streaming over it. His frowning face, lit from below, was peering intently at the flame.

"Not very good," he said. "It might last a minute. Quick, I'm going to throw you the matches and you've got to find them before it goes out. One, two, three, go!"

Emma scrabbled and picked up the precious box. The curious flame still burned.

"Now this," said Roddy. It was a stone wrapped in a rag, which dodged into black shadow. Emma found it just as the light died to a faint red glow and vanished completely.

"What is it?" she said. "What did you light?"

"Bit of my shirt. You've got the rest. But I've been sweating like a pig and some of it's not dry enough to burn. Have you still got the torch?"

"Yes."

"Right, take the battery out and use the boat hook to bash in the side reflector. Then you can find a dry bit of shirt and put it in and light it — it'll protect the flame from the draft. I built myself a little sort of hearth up here, but it wasn't very good."

Emma did as she was told, though it was harder than Roddy made it sound. She was too weak to tear the shirt, so had to light a match while Roddy threw her his knife, and then two more to find the knife by, but it was done in the end and the flame lit the inner wall of the crevasse.

"Right," said Roddy in a gasping voice. "Here goes."

"No, wait," said Emma. There was a crack in that wall which she had stood in, and now she could see it. She worked out over the gap, back against one wall and feet against the other, and as the flame died she wedged the butt of the boat hook into the crack and settled the hook against the other side, pulling down as hard as she could. Then she worked back in the dark, found the torch, now too hot to touch so that she had to empty the ash out by holding it with her jersey, and lit another square of rag.

The boat hook lay like a rigid bar across the crack.

"*That's* better," said Roddy. His legs came over the edge of the rock, blind and groping. Emma talked to him, coaxing him on, watching every move. She had another square of shirt ready as the flames died; now his whole body was clinging to the wall; in the eerie light she could see the sweat streaming down his cheeks; but still he managed to keep moving. His left foot reached the boat hook. "Now!" he cried, and hurled himself back, letting his body fall with a grunt against the rock behind. Then he inched across, as Emma had done, bringing the boat hook with him.

"Well done," she said. "Well done!"

"It's all in the mind," he whispered, shivering as if he had malaria. She took him by the hand, picked up the torch, using her jersey to protect her hand from the heat, and led him over the uneven floor. Twice they had to stop to light fresh squares of shirt before they stood at the bottom of the crack and stared upwards.

"We can chimney up there," said Roddy, hooking the boat hook into his belt.

As he spoke, the light changed. At the very top, blinding, a gold bar lanced from side to side, unwavering, flooding the hole with its glory.

"I'm all right going *up*," said Roddy, and led the way.

It took them almost an hour. The bar of sunlight thinned and vanished, and then a new one shot through another hole. They learned not to look up, because the dazzle of light made it impossible to see their way clearly down in the shadows of the pit. When they did reach the top Emma had to wedge herself agonizingly across the hole to provide Roddy with a foothold to work inside the beehive of coarse stones with the boat hook; he bashed out some of the smaller ones, then levered at a large one. As it gave way, the three or four above it fell back thundering into the tunnel. Shaking all over, Emma crawled through the gap and looked out over the misty loch to The Huts and the boathouses and the gaunt projection of Big House. Then she leaned against Darwin's Pimple and sobbed and sobbed.

"I say, you *are* a good guesser," said Roddy.

The Mr. McAndrew who lived at Fertagh answered their knocking in his pajamas, and wheedled and clucked dismay as Roddy told them how they'd been for a night walk but managed to come back on the wrong side of the loch. Mary answered the telephone, unsurprised. Stodgily, they climbed the hill again and wandered down the far slope, careless of adders, Roddy giggling hysterically when he slithered and

161

fell. Finn had come to meet them in the little cove, using the dinghy with the outboard motor. She asked no questions at all as they stammered back over the still, calm, harmless water.

8

"So," wrote Emma, "there was no time to write that morning. Finn found one of her father's sleeping pills, and I ate it. But I went to sleep before we'd finished the argument."

It was after breakfast now, and the day looked like clearing, but Emma was determined to get it all written down before the Jaguar came back from Glasgow. Then it would be there, in words, and nothing could change it.

"In fact I was too sleepy to remember much of the argument," she wrote, "but I remember what it was about . . ."

It was about what to do; what to say to the TV people. Andy and Roddy were on one side, Emma on the other, and Finn neutral. Miss Newcombe was still asleep. Emma's exhausted voice was hoarse and thin.

"But you can't, you can't, you can't," she cried. "As soon as they've shown the program you'll have hordes of people swarming up here —"

"That's the object of the exercise," said Roddy.

"No it's not. You aren't paupers. You're richer than anyone I've ever met. You don't *want* people coming up here. They'll alter the water. They'll alter the fish and the weeds. The whole balance will change. The thing will die. You've *got* to tell them it was all a joke."

"We've been through all this," said Andy. "I am not going to tell them it was all a joke."

He was being very quiet and patient, and had been since the first white-lipped fury was over, once the children had persuaded him that their story was true.

"*I'll* tell them," said Emma.

"That won't do any good," said Roddy. "They'll expect someone to say that anyway. A bit of controversy's meat and drink to them. Do the mysterious waters . . ."

"I'll show them *Anadyomene*," said Emma.

"That's the point," said Finn. "You can't persuade them my film was a joke, Cousin Emma, unless you can show them how it was taken. Roddy and Andy can't put on another peformance without getting Anna out of the cave. So that's the first thing for all three of you. You don't even know if you can. Now, listen: Andy and Roddy can go back to this cave with some car batteries, and have a go at getting Anna out —"

"They'll be here hours before then," said Andy. "They'll want to know where *I* am, let alone where the monster is. If they see us messing around with a derelict sub on the far side of the loch . . ."

"I've got a toothache," said Finn patiently. "It is agonizing. You've rushed me in to Fort William. Roddy had an appointment anyway, so you took him too. We will have left Poop behind to show them the monster, only she'll somehow have got the idea that it's in Loch Goig. If Poop really dresses up to seduce them, she'll get them out there in a flash. And once they've spent a day with her they'll find it quite easy to believe that she made a little muddle."

"Seeing it's all Roddy's fault . . ." Andy began.

"Shut up," said Finn. "We've finished all that. The only problem is can Roddy manage?"

"He'll have to," said Andy.

"It's a lot of down, from what they told us," said Finn. "Roddy?"

"I'll have a go," said Roddy. "I'm the only one who knows the way."

Even through her humming tiredness Emma could hear that he was already locked with terror — stiff at the idea of that first drop into the dark, and then those innumerable leaps and slithers, and finally the small green target of *Anadyomene*'s hull. He would never make it. And yet she had to get the submarine out, to show the TV people.

"I'll go," she heard her voice saying. "I know the way too. Only I'll have to have a sleep first."

"No time for that," said Andy.

"Rubbish," said Finn. "You can see she's got to. And you've got quite a lot of arrangements to make. You can give her four hours. And another thing, if Roddy runs the big boat, I'll be able to . . ."

165

And then Emma was being shaken awake again, by Finn this time.

"Eleven o'clock," she said. "We've got to get you clear across the loch before they come. Do you really think you can face it?"

"I'll have to," said Emma. Somehow in her sleep she had made up her mind what to do, and how to do it, but she couldn't tell anyone, not even Finn. She staggered off to the bathroom.

On her her way back, for luck, she looked into Miss Newcombe's room. Her goddess was concentrating, like a scholar staring through his magnifying glass at a strange parchment; what she was studying was her own face, reflected three times in a dressing-table mirror. Beside her elbow a flat leather case lay open. Tiptoeing across, Emma saw that it was the most elaborate makeup kit you could imagine, almost a laboratory of beauty, silver-topped jars and phials nestling each into its own nook of satin, just as the lenses had nestled in the box in the darkroom.

"Oh, how lovely!" exlaimed Emma. "I'd love to have something like that. Did someone give it to you?"

Miss Newcombe turned, dazzling. A faint blush seemed to flow under the delicate film of makeup.

"I . . . I *found* it," she said. "I'll try and find you one . . . next time I . . . go somewhere. Did-you-know-there-was-a-monster-in-Loch-Goig-isn't-that-interesting?"

Emma asked Andy about it while they lay in the adder-riddled heather halfway up to Darwin's Pimple. Finn, in the woods above the road, had started Ewan's chain saw and its noise ripped the valley. That was the signal, so

166

Andy had calmly tucked his yoke of batteries away, taken Emma's load and hidden that too, then pulled her down beside him. They watched two cars slide along the road, one yellow, one black. The people who climbed out of them were too small to distinguish, though one did look unusually large; but there was no mistaking Miss Newcombe's turquoise trouser suit as she came down the steps to meet them.

"Will she really be able to stick to her story without getting in a muddle?" said Emma.

"Oh, yes, that's her trouble. She's too teachable. She specialized in lifting things from places like Aspreys in Bond Street with a gang — two men and another woman — who coached her. Nobody — I mean policemen and magistrates and people like that — nobody would believe she didn't know what she was up to, because the stories were clever and you couldn't catch her out once she'd learned them. It was a prison psychiatrist who found out, and Poop's mother, who's a charming lady but hopelessly vague and useless and always getting divorced, asked Father what to do, and Father knew a man at the Home Office — Father always knows a man somewhere — and he sort of went bail for her. She's got a record, but we've guaranteed to keep her out of trouble. Trust Roddy to let her off the leash in Edinburgh. If I'd —"

"Andy," interrupted Emma.

"Unh?"

"The feud's off. That's part of the deal. I was too tired to tell you."

"You were pretty hysterical. What feud?"

"You and Roddy."

"Oh, that. That doesn't mean anything."

"Yes it does. I don't really want to help you, but I'm doing it for two reasons. One is that Roddy couldn't have got *Anadyomene* stuck without me. The other is that you're going to promise to call the feud off. Roddy's promised — that's why I went out with him at all. Now you're going to promise. I hope."

(After all, Emma reasoned, she must let Andy think she had a motive for helping him, or he mightn't let her crew with Ewan — everything depended on that. If he thought she'd been hysterical the night before, so much the better. Also, it would mean she kept her bargain with Roddy, even if later she was going to betray the whole family. Some things are more important than others, but you look after the little things as well if you can manage it.)

"OK," said Andy, without thinking about it.

"That's not good enough," said Emma. "How do I know you'll stick to it? You're all such liars. What do McAndrews make *each other* swear by?"

Andy rolled on his side in the heather and smiled at her. At once she could see why the girls who ran across him in a good mood at Edinburgh University found it difficult to concentrate upon their studies.

"I'll stick to it because I like you," he said. "We can't have the Tuppers of the world thinking worse of us, can we? Oh, great, Poop's taking them straight off — I thought we were going to have to stick around here while McTurdle drank five whiskies. I bet he's spotted the champagne Mary put in with the picnic."

Working with Andy, Emma could understand how the Scots had conquered whole empires for the English.

Though he was prepared to embark on the maddest enterprise for a whim, once his pride was engaged he worked like a slave to bring it off. And he had thought it all out; he had brought the right ropes and pegs and slings to lower them down the shaft with their load, so that they were down safe and easy in twenty minutes compared with the slogging hour she'd taken to climb it that morning. And he was strong, moving easily with his half-hundredweight yoke of batteries over the treacherous rocks, while Emma carried the torch and the spare torch and a coil of cable and another coil of rope and the satchel of tools and spikes. She was glad of the rest when Andy lowered his yoke at the place where the crevasse widened.

"You mean you got Roddy down that!" he said.

"He got himself down," said Emma stubbornly.

Andy only grunted.

"Isn't there anything *you're* afraid of?" said Emma. "The same way Roddy is of heights. I'm terrified of snakes, for instance, and . . ."

But she couldn't talk about her fear of being trapped in *Anadyomene,* with the bottomless cold deeps waiting to receive her. In any case, Andy just grunted again, took the tools, and working across the crevasse made a slanting ladder of spikes, up which he climbed with the end of the rope. Emma put the batteries one by one into the sling and he hauled them up. They rested again at the top. Five minutes later they were out of the tunnel into the heat and stench at the back of the cave. Emma flashed her torch among the rocks at their feet.

"This way," she said.

"Sure? It's easy to make a mistake in a jumble like this."

"Roddy made a pointer."

She showed him the little pile of stones, shaped like an arrowhead, on the flat rock.

"He did several of those," she said. "Anywhere he thought we might get lost on our way back."

"Bless his angry heart," said Andy, settling the yoke of batteries onto the ground. "There's nothing wrong with him, but sometimes I know just how Romulus felt when Remus jumped over that wall of his."

He put out his foot to scatter the pile, then withdrew it and laughed and took the torch. As he flashed the long beam across the ridges of the roof the hidden pack bayed its terror, a shock of sound that made Emma reach out and force his hand down. This was a big, rubber-cased torch with only one switch position. The noise died away and Andy gave a long, shuddering sigh.

"I didn't believe it," he said. "I didn't honestly believe it."

They moved on, Emma keeping the beam as much as she could on the ground, lighting Andy across the ledges; the steamy reek filled her lungs and the heat made her blouse stick and suck at her ribs and shoulders. Going down became an effort like going up had been — it was moving against the current, the draft of foul air, the current of dread. They said very little. Sometimes, inevitably, the light shone out across the cave, and the creatures down by the water yelped their agony. Next time they rested Andy took the torch.

"Now listen," he said. "You've got to let me have a look. We've got something here that doesn't exist anywhere else in the world. We can't make sensible decisions about it unless we know what it consists of."

"But —"

"Cousin Emma, I am going to have a look. You can hide your eyes if you want to."

"No. I want to see too. Only, Andy, please don't make it longer than you have to."

She stood beside him on the ledge and he swung the beam out and down. As the screeching echoes filled her skull he flicked it off the water and began to play it along the wet rocks at the edge where the nests were. The moving circle peeled the creatures into the water, unzipped them from the rocks in white foam. They were gone too quick to see, except where the small ones floundered up the slope of weed, but by looking just in front of where the main light moved Emma could see the adults preparing themselves for the leap, clumsier on land even than seals. Ruthlessly Andy played the beam all the way round the dark lake. On the far side its light was too faint to show anything except the glimmering splashes of the dives. When at last he switched the light off the yelling took a long time to die. It was as though the creatures knew he had done it on purpose.

"Well," he said quietly, "if you could put on a show like that three times a day, people would come from all over the world to see it."

Emma said nothing. In the new dark she saw that there was in fact an element of light, a green, wavering blur down to her left, just where *Anadyomene* lay moored — daylight seeping through the water from the loch outside.

"It wasn't a tunnel," she said. "More of a slit, but this is the widest end."

"If you got in with the head on," said Andy, "we should be able to get out with it off easy enough. Provided twenty-four volts will turn the engine, that is. Let's sit down. I feel like a smoke."

There were a couple of yelps as his lighter flared, and all the time the welter and splash of the creatures scrambling back to their nests.

"So that's it," said Emma, after a while.

"What's what?" said Andy. "Title of a Directory of Famous Inanimate Objects."

"They ought to be bigger than they are," said Emma. "The book says that the dinosaurs could stand short cold spells because they were so huge that they contained enough warmth to put up with some heat loss — is that right?"

"It makes sense, mechanically speaking."

"But Roddy told me there were a lot of volcanoes around here, which must be why there are still hot springs. I expect they were hotter once, and when the Ice Ages came the creatures found this cave and learned to live in here. They could go outside to hunt under the ice —"

"Not much to hunt," said Andy. "The ice cap covered the mountains in Scotland."

"But the springs might have been hot enough to keep it melted here," said Emma. "You got hot lakes in Greenland, I know. But they'd get so used to living in the dark that their skins wouldn't protect them against the sun any more, and so they'd become afraid of all light. And they could afford to get smaller because they had this heat to come back to."

Andy stubbed out his cheroot and stood up.

"Come on," he said. "Switch on that light, Cousin Emma, and let's get cracking. You don't seem to appreciate that in her way Anna is just as interesting as these stinking reptiles."

"No she's not!" said Emma. "Monsieur Goubet's original boat would be *quite* interesting, but nothing like the creatures. Nothing. And Anna's only a steal."

"You're an unsophisticated Botswanan. Fakes fetch more at Sotheby's than originals these days."

Emma started to say something about Andy having tried to fake a monster, but made a muddle of it. As she led him down the ledges she began to wonder whether the volcanoes had not only provided the hot springs but also made the cave. Eigg had been a volcano, and all huge Skye, and Ardnamurchan. Perhaps some uprush of lava had forced the mountains apart and left these passages, this vast bubble. Not a bronze bubble like *Anadyomene,* enduring a few pounds of pressure for a few hours, but a stone bubble that had stayed hidden here since long before Man chipped his first tools in the Olduvai Gorge. A bubble that had become the home of the last of the great lizards.

As they came to the lower ledges it was impossible to hide the torch beam; again the long yelp rose, and again the creatures exploded into the water from the rimming rocks. She even saw the bigger splash of the furthest one as it plunged down on *Anadyomene*'s hull, too stupid to have learned. It might take a whole generation before the creatures discovered that that was not a good place to dive from. No, they could adapt no further. And the whole earth was changing. It would be astonishing if they survived another hundred years, unless . . .

Anadyomene, brave absurdity, had stood up well to being dived on. The arch of fiber glass, that had seemed so lifelike until Emma had seen the real thing, rose above her, horribly tattered over one eye by the rough passage into the cave. Emma switched on the other torch and played both beams around the hull while Andy strove and contrived with the batteries. It took him some time, and all the while the yelling tore at her ears. Then he unbolted the fiber-glass head and cut a big V-shaped notch in its neck with a saw, snipping through the supporting frame with wire cutters. He judged it just right, so that by pressing the sides of the V together he was able to cram the fiber glass down, headfirst, through the hatch. At last he stood up and made signs to Emma; with a shaking hand she threw him the larger torch, which he caught easily; then, while he slid its beam to and fro over the water she lowered herself down the mooring rope, stepped onto the deck, and slipped into the hatch. The air inside was unbelievably bad.

The hull rocked as Andy cut the taut rope. The hatch clicked above her in the sudden silence — a silence, after that noise, as thick and heavy as deafness. She shook her head as though her ears were full of water. Then a strangeness struck her.

"Why don't you turn the light on?" she said, as she watched Andy kneel by torchlight and begin to measure the cables for the batteries. He shook his head.

"No go," he said. "The batteries are dead — I tried 'em. You and Roddy put such a strain on them that a couple of cells must have gone futt — I told you they were on their last legs and searchlights *eat* juice — and since then the rest of the cells have simply been shorting out through the dud ones. I don't like it. We've got twenty-four volts in the batteries I've brought, which would have done us with the bit of juice left in the old ones, but without that . . . Ah well, we'll just have to see."

Emma settled back in her chair and thought. She didn't like it either. Above all terrors, she feared most the thought of getting stuck under the ledge of rock. To sit there in this bronze coffin, with the warm springs drifting past them and the creatures going out and in. . . .

"Well, we'll give it a go," said Andy. "We can always go back and say sorry. Cousin Emma, you asked me what I'm afraid of, the way Roddy's afraid of climbing down. I'll tell you, I'm afraid of making a fool of myself in public, that's what. Ready, motor on."

"How fast?"

"Won't make much difference. If you put it to full we'll still go slow."

The blue spark looked all right, but the engine note climbed painfully slow from its bass grind, and began to level off when it was nowhere near its proper hum.

"Motor off," snapped Andy. "I don't like it. Finn's going to get the frogmen up from Helensburgh if we're not out by six, but even if they come by helicopter they won't be here before nine. We won't last that long in this air. OK, we'll go back and face the music. The monster will fail to surface, and we'll leave the telly folk with a mystery."

A mystery was the last thing Emma wanted.

"Andy?"

"Yeah?"

"I was thinking just now, while you were connecting the batteries. The hot springs are in the cave, but their water gets out into the loch. There must be a current, and it must go through the slit. If you've got enough juice to circle around to the right place, I don't see why we shouldn't just drift out. If we're cunning with the pumps, I mean, and submerge just far enough. We pumped ourselves up and down several times last night, but the head kept catching before the current had time to move us."

Andy thought about it.

"OK," he said at last. "We'll submerge here, using the stopcocks, because that means I'll be able to see a bit, and besides this hull's got less resistance underwater. Then I'll try and take us around till we're a few feet away from the entrance, and if we decide we're not drifting fast enough we can surface. You prepared to risk it?"

"Yes," whispered Emma.

"OK. Flood tanks for ten. . . . Off. . . . Level OK? . . . Two strokes on the pumps. . . . Motor on — whoops, she's a sow at this speed, don't bother with the hydroplanes, they won't bite. . . . Motor off. . . . Hydroplanes full up, hard! . . . Ease them slowly back . . . good girl. Right, what's happening? I think we're moving, a bit sideways, but you can't have everything. . . . Two on the pumps. . . . We're in!"

It took them thirty-seven minutes by Andy's watch to drift the few yards under the curtain of rock. They scraped, at different times, both top and bottom, but never both together; they never quite achieved the exact balance between floating and sinking — even half a stroke on the pumps was enough to make the difference — so they were endlessly busy with tiny adjustments; the air became so bad that Emma found herself constantly yawning, and not with tiredness, though she was tired enough in all conscience. After a while she was able to see the rock roof drift by through her own observation port, now that it was no longer hidden by the beast's neck; she looked for the ridge on which they had snagged last night, but couldn't see it. And then, heavy and staggering, she was shoving the pump levers to and fro. The light through the glass became a blaze of day. The hatch was open, the sweet air of late afternoon pouring in, and Roddy was calling the news of the telly folks' deception from the deck of the launch.

Finn and Mary had moved every scrap of Emma's belongings out of her room to make way for Mr. McTurdle. Emma staggered up to Andy Coaches' flat above the old stables, where Mrs. Andy (who spoke no English at all) smiled happily at the few words of Gaelic which Caitlin had taught Emma, gave her a high tea, and put her to bed. She slept for fourteen hours.

And then, after sneaking through the heavenly smelling pinewoods to the bay beyond the point, she was again encased in the bronze bubble, again turning taps, shoving at pump levers, starting the motor, listening to Ewan muttering over his stopwatch and compass, wondering whether he would notice any difference about the way the boat was running, with the tail so much more buoyant than it was supposed to be. She thought that all that would happen was that they would emerge from the water a bit short of their target area, because the extra tilt of the hydroplanes to keep the boat level would increase its water resistance. On the other hand she had risked a notch more engine speed than usual, to make up for it, and the bubble in the tube was reasonably obedient. Her mouth was very dry, and she gulped nervously, not at the idea of danger but like going onstage in front of the whole school for the form plays. If it didn't work she would simply seek out this Mr. Gritt and show him *Anadyomene* and tell him the whole story.

"Ah, well," said Ewan at last. "I'm not very fond of Glasgow folk. Up we go, Miss Emma."

Emma thought of the group on the shore, poised and waiting, all eyes straining for the wrong place because the McAndrews thought it would look better if one of the cameramen or someone noticed the surge of the repaired head out of the water before it had to be pointed out to them. Ewan would now be peering through his slot, tense for the moment when water became air and they had to level out before the hull showed; she allowed the bubble in the tube to creep aft.

"We're up," he said, and paused. "But it's a queer thing, we're a wee bit short. Maybe those other batteries haven't the power in them." (All the McAndrews knew that Roddy and Emma had taken *Anadyomene* out at night, got her stuck, and then run out of electricity. There was no need to tell them about the cave or the creatures.)

Firmly, Emma pulled the hydroplane lever towards her and with her other hand slowed the motor — the last thing she wanted was to force the submarine into a dive.

"The motor doesn't sound too good," she said loudly, hoping to excuse and at the same time cover the change of note. "I hope it'll be strong enough to get us home, Ewan. . . ."

Now, she said to herself. Now! Happen!

"There's a queer thing," began Ewan, when it happened.

She had heard it before — the hull juddering and groaning as the engine slowed. Emma flung the control into neutral and collapsed in her seat, panting as though she'd climbed a hill.

"There's a thing," said Ewan. "What do you fancy made that happen?"

"We've caught the propeller in the tail," said Emma. "Andy did it once, so it's not your fault."

(And that was true.)

"I was beginning to think we were sitting queerly. Had you been looking at the level?"

"No. Sorry. I don't have to when we're on the surface. What shall we do now?"

"Shall we be submerging, do you think?"

"No thank you!" said Emma. "Over the gulf, with no engine! The whole joke's over, I'm afraid. It's a pity — it was a good joke, but not worth drowning for."

"Agreed," said Ewan solemnly. "Shall we pump her twenty, then. My, but there's the launch coming out — will you face them first, Miss Emma? Mr. Andy will not be very pleased with us."

"No," said Emma, "why should I — I'm not even a Mc-Andrew. You go first. You're grown-up."

"You do not think the television men would prefer to see a pretty lassie's face coming out?"

"No, I don't. Talk to them in the Gaelic and perhaps they'll still think you're a monster of a sort." She sounded as sulky as she could. The important thing was to get Ewan's head out of the hatch while she opened the stop-cocks to blow the tanks level. She had managed to sneak a few missed strokes into her pumping, but not nearly enough to compensate for the buoyancy already there. If Andy found the craft trimmed like this when he got her to shore, he'd know just what had happened.

The noise of water rippling faintly along the hull changed to the underwater drub of the launch's engine.

"Ah well," said Ewan again, sheepish with shyness. The hull rocked with the coming of the launch, and rocked again as Ewan stood on his seat to raise the hatch. The bronze bubble flooded with lovely sunlight, blocked out as Ewan's big shoulders went through the hatch. Emma suddenly realized that in five minutes she would never need to sit in this trap again. With a sigh of pleasure she crept aft to the stopcocks.

Then everything changed.

Anadyomene shook and plunged, as she had when the creature had dived on her in the cave. The hull tilted with a roaring noise, Emma lost her footing and tumbled back to her chair; a huge cold force was pouring over her, pinning her in; it was dark. She heard the after batteries crash loose on her right. . . .

The drill which her dread had practiced ordered her hands. Without thought she scrabbled the catch up and wrenched at the little wheel; it was stiff, but moved; she flung all her strength into turning it, once round, twice, three times. Something gave, and outside the hull she heard one dull clunk.

She knelt on the now horizontal back of her seat and let her breath go. She was kneeling in water. She had been turning the wheel under water. The water was not coming up. Her ears were not popping with increased pressure. If they were still sinking, they were not sinking fast. Perhaps, with the weight released, they were even going up. *Anadyomene* was a bronze bubble, and now it was half full of water. It was poised in the loch, with the hatch open, bows downward, with a pocket of air trapped in the stern end;

180

Emma was kneeling on the back of a chair, breathing that air.

If the hull was now floating up, she must stay where she was until it reached the surface. It might start to tilt there, in which case she must scramble out as best she could before more water started to crash in as the pocket of air escaped. If the hull was sinking, she must go now.

She knew she would never make it. She was not a good enough swimmer. So they would *have* to be going up — it was the only hope.

As she poised herself to be ready for the first sign of tilting, she saw below her in the water the faint round of the hatch, lit by the sun outside, seeping through the water. Something touched the hull beside her, but she paid no attention — she would be able to tell whether she was floating or sinking by whether that round got lighter or darker.

It got darker. Suddenly. Blanked out. The water gurgled beside her.

"Emma darling," said a gasping voice.

"I'm here."

"Oh, super. We thought you might . . . they've got her by the tail, but it's almost pulling the launch under. Quick. I can't take you out through that hole, both together. You'll have to pull yourself out and then I'll take you up, but you'll have to be quick, or *I* won't have any breath left. Hurry! Something's happened!"

Emma too had felt the jerk. She took one big breath, leaned down into the water, twisting sideways, grasped the edge of the hatch, and pulled herself violently down. As she was trying to kick herself through from the top of the chair, something grasped at her hair and pulled; a bubble flooded from her lips, the pain in her scalp stopped, and there were hands under her shoulders and her chest was rasping against the hatchway, then her thighs. By an effort of will she forced herself into limpness and began to count. Count and lie still in the heavy, drumming redness. Still. Count. If you can reach thirty you can reach forty. Emma! In the redness. In the blackness . . .

Tock went the drugged woodpecker. *Clack,* it snicked. *Clack. Tock.* Emma opened her eyes and looked at the ceiling of her room in The Huts. Her throat was sore, and her chest felt as though someone had been leaning on it with enormous weights.

Clack. Tock. Suddenly the sounds made sense.

"Miss Newcombe."

She tried to call the name but only managed a harsh whisper. Carefully, she worked the saliva up in her mouth, swallowed it, waited on the rhythm of the clicks, and tried again.

"Miss Newcombe!"

A chair shuffled, and then the gold head poked through her window.

"Was that you calling, darling? I hope I didn't wake you up."

"It's all right," said Emma huskily. "Ask him to come home. Tell him it's important. Urgent. I heard you writing your letter."

"Urgent?" said Miss Newcombe eagerly.

"Yes."

"Really urgent?"

"Yes."

"I've got a telegram, you see. It says 'Come home. Ur-

182

gent.' And his address. He gave it to me before he left. Is it urgent enough for that?"

"I think so."

"Oh, super. I'll drive into Mallaig and send it, and that means I needn't write this beastly letter. Are you sure it's all right? He won't be angry about being taken away from his beetles?"

"It's all right."

"Super."

Emma shut her eyes.

"Emma, darling," whispered the delicious voice, as though it were afraid to wake her.

"Unh?"

"People . . . when they've . . . saved people's lives . . . they're allowed to ask people . . . for things . . . I-hope-you-don't-mind."

"I haven't got very much," said Emma through her scraping throat. "But I'll give it all to you. All."

"Oh I don't mean *that* sort of thing. People are always giving me *that* sort of thing. But will you go on calling me Miss Newcombe? *That's* what I like. Nobody else does that. Nobody. Not counting magistrates."

"I'll make up for them all."

"Super. I'll go and send the telegram."

Yes, thought Emma, listening drowsily to the feet scampering across the hessian matting of the verandah. It's like being called Cousin Emma all the time, instead of just Emma, to remind you that you don't really belong. Even by Finn.

Finn was her next visitor. It must have been hours later, because the light was different.

"Good-oh," she said as she edged through the door. "I've got a present for you, but I couldn't give it you while the boys were here and I didn't want to wake you up."

"Where are they?"

"Putting a sort of door into Darwin's Pimple and measuring how much ladder they'll need to reach the bottom of the drop. They want to hold a press conference, but the business this morning has slightly queered their pitch with the news media. Here's your present.

She tossed a flat, round tin onto the bed, then settled herself at the foot of it, nursing in her lap a black, tubular, many-knobbed gadget. Part of one of her cameras, Emma thought.

"You'll have to explain," she said. "Nobody's told me what happened. Where are the TV people? What happened to *Anadyomene?*"

"Anna sank," said Finn. "She's in the gulf. It was all Mr. McTurdle's fault, jumping onto the hull to give the cameras a funny shot, when Andy kept shouting to him not to. That shoved the nose under and she started to fill, and the more she filled the quicker she went; Ewan nipped out, but the telly folk were all busy rescuing that fat oaf McTurdle, and everybody was shouting. But Roddy caught hold of the tail, and that started to pull the launch under, and then it eased — Andy thought you'd got the weight off . . ."

"Yes."

"And there we were. You weren't very far down, but it was ages before the telly folk grasped that there was somebody still down there, because they were all in such furious tempers with each other. We could actually see Anna hanging there, so Poop undressed and went down to investigate, and we saw her go into the hatch, and then the tail broke. I was sick, literally sick. I vomited. But she got you out. We saw you both coming up long after we couldn't see Anna any more. You were like a corpse, and even Poop was more dead than alive. And do you know, all this time both cameras, the one on the shore and the one on the launch, never stopped filming — just as though it was a sort of play which would all come all right in the end."

"Yes. I'll tell you what happened in the boat when my voice is better. What's this?"

Emma patted the flat tin.

"Film. They took miles of it. There was a lot of useless stuff about Loch Goig, with Poop looking windblown. Then one of the cameramen, the arty one, fell in love with Big House and took reels of that, and there was all the stuff about the rescue, and an interview with Andy Ghillie, and other bits and bobs. But there was only one bit which showed our monster looking at all like a monster, because you came up in the wrong place and the launch was in the way of the shore camera. Gabriella knows I'm mad about cameras, so she asked the cameramen to let me hang around. That's why I was there when they were sorting out what they'd got, and I kept my eye on where they put it and how it was numbered. When they were packing up I told Poop what I wanted, and she went and what she calls *found* it for me."

"So they can't even make a pretend mystery," croaked Emma. "I was worrying about that. Except they've still got *your* bit of film."

"That's copyright," said Finn. "I rang up Old Crow, and he sicced a lawyer onto them. Then Gabriella rang up to

185

say they're showing five minutes of the hoax that went wrong and the daring rescue this evening. Nice of her, considering. In fact she came out of it pretty well. She'd told Gritt and McTurdle all along it was a hoax, and she was the only one who didn't lose her temper."

"I'd like to have met her."

"You will," said Finn, caressing the object in her lap and then holding it up. "I'm afraid I gave Poop the idea that she could *find* anything she fancied, and just after the telly folk went, Mary brought me this. It's three-hundred-and-twenty-quids-worth of telephoto lens. I told Gabriella that it had somehow got left out in the packing and why didn't she drive up this weekend and fetch it. She said yes. Andy'll purr, won't he?"

"I hope so."

"So do I. Now I'll go and see if I can find something for your throat. I'm afraid our medicine cupboard is rather randomly labeled, so you won't mind if it turns out to be stuff for cows' udders, will you?"

The telephone rang just as Emma was going through the hall in her dressing gown to watch herself being rescued. She picked the receiver up and said the number. The stuff Finn had found in the medicine cupboard, even if it was meant for cows' udders, had done wonders.

"One moment," said the operator. "Are you there, Switzerland? You're through."

"All right," said a man's voice, dry and angry. "Where is she?"

"In the bottom of the loch," gabbled Emma.

"No!" cried the voice, then paused. "People do not send

telegrams from the bottom of my loch, not even Poop. To whom have I the honor of speaking at this absurd expense?"

"Emma Tupper. I asked Miss Newcombe to send the telegram. That's Major McAndrew, isn't it?"

"It is. Nick Tupper's girl?"

"Yes."

"Hmm. Your father spoke fairly well of you. What's all this about? Who's at the bottom of the loch?"

"*Anadyomene.* No other *people.*"

"You're talking in code, girl. Will you please explain to me why I must come home."

"We've found something. An animal. It oughtn't to be alive, but it is."

"Ah. How many legs?"

"None. Flippers."

"Yes. Yes. I see. There's a plane leaves tomorrow morning. I hate night flights."

"Major McAndrew?"

"What else?"

"The boys are making plans. If you could send a telegram . . ."

"That'll help you stave them off till I come. The U.S. Calvary gallops over the horizon to rescue the beleaguered garrison. Finn on your side?"

"She *says* she's neutral."

"They're the dangerous ones. Well, I'll be interested to meet you, *ma cousine.*"

Emma reached the drawing room in time to see herself being hauled inert from the water, while bearded cameramen queued to give the kiss of life to Miss Newcombe. The

McAndrews were analyzing the awfulness of Mr. Mc-
Turdle when Mary coughed at the door.

"They have rung through a telegram, Master Andy," she
said. "Himself will be coming home the morn, and will you
meet him at Glasgow airport at half-past two?"

9

There was no point in writing any more. Dully,
Emma leafed through the diary, wondering what
to do. Sleep hadn't helped her make up her mind.
She had gone to bed with the vague idea of get-
ting Miss Newcombe to drive her off to Mallaig
and posting the diary to Daddy, just like that. But
now she saw that that would put Daddy in a fix,
the same fix that she was in: nothing could be
done — that is, nothing could be done and leave
you feeling that you'd done right — unless Major
McAndrew agreed.

She shut the folder and looked just as dully out
at the loch. It was a nice enough day, but . . .
Anyway, she was glad that it had cleared up yes-
terday in time to sparkle for his homecoming.

189

He was smaller than Emma expected, barely taller than Finn; thin, tanned and dapper, with a spruce little white moustache. His hair had gone back a little from his forehead, but not enough to make him seem at all bald; it was not quite white, but flecked with darker gray that made it easy to believe that it had once been as black as Andy's and Roddy's. He held himself like a soldier, a man used to horseback, but he didn't look quite like a soldier. He didn't look quite like a scholar either, though — but it was easy to see why Roddy said he was a spy. You could imagine him plotting quietly in tents with Arab princes. Only his eyes showed how tired he was with travel. Miss Newcombe spanieled around him. His hand was cold and dry when Emma shook it.

"How do you do?" said Emma, very nervous.

"How do you do?" he said. "How good it is to hear those words! In Geneva nobody seems to say anything except 'Gladda meecha' when they are introduced. Mary, my dear, there still seem to be three of my offspring in tolerable health. None missing. You've done well."

He kissed Mary on the cheek, asked Caitlin about her aunt's hip, said something else to Jeannie, called good-night to Andy Coaches and a greeting in the Gaelic to the four or five other McAndrews who seemed for no special reason to be lounging on the road between The Huts and the loch.

"In Grandfather's day there'd have been a piper when the Chief came home," whispered Finn. "Father can't stand any of that nonsense."

"I have my own brand of nonsense," said Major McAndrew without looking around. "Perhaps Mary will be kind enough to bring us a drink, and we'll sit and look at the evening for a while."

There was a chair on the verandah that hadn't been there before; he settled himself slowly into it and looked in silence at his own slim foot. Miss Newcombe cuddled herself onto a cushion on the floor beside him. Roddy, astoundingly, brought a deck chair for Emma. Mary returned with a silver tray, glasses, Coke, and a bottle of champagne dewy with chill. Emma watched her strong, small fingers coping with the cork.

"Quiet, now," said Major McAndrew, holding up his hand. It was as though he had commanded silence on the whole rain-freshened valley, and the whole valley, being his, had obeyed; cliff and scree, pine and heather, and the long reaches of the loch waited poised in stillness.

Pop! went Mary's cork, and the foam flowed. Major McAndrew's hand stayed up. His lips were moving. He was counting.

Pop answered the cliff at last, incredibly soft and far, but still the same noise flung back.

"Good omen," said Major McAndrew, smiling and ruffling Miss Newcombe's hair. "That's my sort of nonsense."

Mary took the glasses around.

"Actually," said Roddy, "we have a little man up there with binoculars, who bursts a balloon when he sees Mary pull the cork out. Anything to keep Father happy."

"It's too far," said Emma, puzzled. "The pop wasn't loud enough to get there and back."

"The cliff is curved, like a lens," said Major McAndrew. "You might not even be able to hear the noise out there, because the sound-waves have spread and thinned, but the curve sends them back to this point, like a focus, and you can hear them again. That's why my father built his laboratory at this point. That was *his* sort of nonsense. We will talk about your troubles after supper, Cousin Emma."

There were candles, of course, and old, old silver, silky clean. And an extra course, a bitter savory. And then peaches, which Andy and Miss Newcombe had bought in Glasgow. The Major said his stomach was too delicate for red wine but he seemed to knock back a lot of the white, first the champagne, then hock, then a yellow wine from Bordeaux with the peaches. Emma had a glass of this, sweet and polleny. It was thirty-five years old, past its best the Major said. Even so it seemed to be an extraordinary thing to be *destroying* it by pouring it down your throat, something so old, made with such care. She tried to remember the taste of every sip, as though she were putting it away on a shelf in her library.

The McAndrews were less rowdy than usual, but their humor was wilder. A mad, elaborate scheme was devised for kidnapping the prime minister and substituting Mr. Crowe, disguised, for him. Mr. Crowe would then pilot a bill through Parliament making the use of liniment compulsory for all bald Englishmen. Major McAndrew smiled and sipped and listened, occasionally making dry, ridiculous objections.

"But are you really going to be *poor?*" said Miss Newcombe at last. "Will I have to, er, work again?"

"I hope not," said Major McAndrew. "It looks as though the company will have to be wound up, but it has quite a

lot of assets, and my father made a number of more ortho-
dox investments, which have done reasonably well over the
year. We shall be able to live on fat for a while. . . ."

"Fat!" said Miss Newcombe, startled.

"It is a way of saying that I am still able to keep you in
the manner to which you are accustomed."

"Super," said Miss Newcombe. "Then everything's all
right."

"Not exactly," said Major McAndrew. "I now call the
meeting to order. Andy has given me, in the car, an outline
of all that has happened. I now move the motion that we
should all regard the various idiocies involved as over and
done with. There will be no recriminations. Does anyone
second the motion?"

"I do," said Andy.

"I put it to the vote. Nem con? Good. But I believe that
Andy has a point to raise which he regards as not covered
by this motion."

"I have," said Andy. "I've been talking to Ewan Uphill
about what happened in the boat before the tail got caught
in the propeller. I could see that Anna was down by the
bows as the launch came up. He told me that she had been
behaving a bit oddly, and that there was a sudden power
loss just after he surfaced, which he attributed to the different set of batteries failing. But those batteries were perfectly good. I gave them a drop test. The only answer is
that Cousin Emma deliberately gave the stern extra buoyancy, and cut the power in order not to drive the boat
under. *She wanted to tangle the propeller.* It had happened by accident the first time she was crew, in much the
same way. As a result of this action, which was deliberate

and not negligent, and so in my view cannot be defined merely as an idiocy, she sank Anna and nearly drowned Poop."

"Unfair!" said Finn.

"She couldn't have known about that fat elephant Mc-Turdle," said Roddy.

"Order," said Major McAndrew. "I think Andy is over-playing his hand. I am sorry to have lost Anna. I should be sorry to lose Poop. But as Roddy says, the particular danger could not have been foreseen. You must learn not to attempt to play upon a chairman's prejudices so barefacedly. Let us see what Cousin Emma has to say."

"On a point of order," said Finn.

"Yes," said Major McAndrew.

"Has Cousin Emma got a vote?"

"I don't think so. No, I'm afraid not."

"Then she's got my vote," said Finn. "I hearby appoint her my proxy in all matters arising."

"Is that in order?" said Andy.

"I don't see why not," said Major McAndrew.

"There's never been anyone like Finn for backing out of responsibilities," said Roddy.

"Cousin Emma," said Major McAndrew. "Would you care to explain your actions to the meeting?"

"It was my fault," said Emma. "Andy's quite right. I did it on purpose. And I ought to have told Ewan what I'd done, and leveled the boat out, and then we'd have stayed floating when the fat man jumped on her. I *ought* to have done that anyway, and not left Ewan thinking it was all his own fault, but I couldn't think of a way of telling him without explaining why I wanted to do it, which would have meant telling him about the creatures."

"But *why?*" said Andy. "It's not just letting us down when you've lived like one of the family. You worked like a horse to get Anna out of the cave. *You* had the notion of drifting her out, and that was a real risk, and you knew it."

"Order," said Major McAndrew. "I must remind you to address all remarks to the chair, and not make personal attacks on other members of the meeting. However, we will take your remarks as so addressed. Cousin Emma?"

"The important thing," said Emma slowly, though she had thought all this out many times, both before and after the accident, "was to get the TV people to go away knowing they had been hoaxed. At first I was just going to try and get Mr. Gritt to come and see Anna tied up in the bay, and show him the head in the woods. But then I realized he might want to know why I wanted to spoil the joke, and I'm — I'm not a very good liar. So I thought if I could make sure that *Anadyomene* came right out of the water during the run. . . . And then I thought that would mean that they didn't have a film of a complete run, with the head going under again, so it would be harder for them to *pretend* they thought it was a real monster."

"Concise and explicit," said Major McAndrew. "And your motive for making them go away?"

"There'd have been a mystery. Even if they hadn't got the film and hadn't seen Anna, there'd still have been a mystery. Hundreds of people would have come pouring up here. There'd have been people like the ones who are looking in Loch Ness and Loch Morar for the monsters there; and they'd be bound to find the creatures pretty soon. And then there'd be the tourists, camping round the loch, filling it with sewage and chemicals. The creatures would have died — they're only *just* alive, though they look so strong and horrid. But one tiny change could kill them and there are bound to be thousands of changes. Look!"

She pointed at the lovely oryx horns on the wall. "Do you know how many of *them* there are left in the world? Less than a hundred. Do you know how many tigers, outside zoos? Less than a thousand. Man kills everything, everything. Sometimes he does it with guns and sometimes with sewage, or oil, or . . ."

She ran out of breath and argument, and sat trembling. Major McAndrew reached for the bottle and refilled her glass.

"Less explicit, but still cogent," he said. "Andy?"

"In a way," said Andy, poking at the tip of the big cigar he'd taken from a box on the table, "in a way I'm glad Emma mucked things up, though I'm sorry to lose Anna. In fact I ought to have arranged it myself, but I'd got the bit between my teeth, and I couldn't quite face it. It didn't turn out so badly, either. So I vote we don't worry about what Emma did or why she did it. The question is —"

"One moment," said Major McAndrew, "I put the motion that Cousin Emma's actions in *Anadyomene,* though not necessarily regarded as idiotic, be included among the idiocies covered by the previous motion. Proposed? Thank you, Andy. Seconded? Thank you, Roddy. Now, Andy, please proceed."

"The question is, how can we make the most of the cave? When I was in France last year I went down the Gouffre de Padirac; there were hundreds of people queuing to see it all day long, and that's only stalactites and things. One advantage of our cave is that it wouldn't cost much to make it easy to get into, down under Darwin's Pimple, and —"

"On a point of order," said Finn, "do I have to revoke my proxy to address the meeting?"

"Nice point," said Major McAndrew. "Let's say not — it'll save time. Proposed? Seconded? Carry on, Finn."

"You know about Lascaux?" said Finn. "Two boys found this cave of Stone Age paintings, thousands of years old, gorgeous. The people who owned the land made a packet out of letting the tourists in. And then the paintings, which had lasted, just as good as ever, all those years when nobody was seeing them, began to flake off the wall, in only a few years. It was the tourists' breath which did it."

"Tourists," said Major McAndrew. "I am interested that Andy is even prepared to tolerate the idea, lucrative though it might be. Ice-cream kiosks. Parking lots. Plastic bags blowing about."

"I've thought about that," said Andy. "They needn't come this side at all — they could go up through Fertagh. Andy Fertagh would put up with anything for a share of the loot. We couldn't stop them looking across here, of course. . . . And about Lascaux. You can go there now — they're screening it all off. We could manage something like that, I'd have thought."

"It isn't just screening the creatures from the people's breath," said Roddy. "We'd have to screen the people from the creatures'. Father and Finn haven't smelled 'em. Anyway, I think Andy's got a scheme there — I'm for it."

"Finn," said Major McAndrew. "This matter of the tourists — you had better revoke your proxy for the moment, as it is more likely to affect you than Cousin Emma."

"I hereby revoke my proxy," said Finn. "I'm against seeing the brutes or letting them see us, even from the top of the hill. My proxy now hereby reverts to Cousin Emma."

"But hey," said Roddy, "You — I mean she was all for the scheme when we were just faking a monster to bring tourists up here."

"I didn't really think it would work," said Finn, "any more than Andy did. I just thought it might keep us out of trouble."

"Some hope," said Roddy.

"It was those telly folk," said Finn, "mooching all over the place as if they belonged. I realized I couldn't stand it."

"Um," said Major McAndrew. "We appear to have a split vote on the question of whether we can stand tourists. Let us put that aside, for the moment, as it is merely ancillary to Andy's main proposal. We have not heard any alternative suggestions, but I am sure Cousin Emma has one. Cousin Emma, supposing the place belonged to you —"

"It does," said Roddy, and explained about the Russian prince and the trouser salesman. Like all spur-of-the-moment fantasies, it didn't go quite so well second time through.

"Not a very strong claim," said Major McAndrew.

"Perhaps we could buy her off by giving her the hill with the cave in it," said Finn.

"If we were to do that," said Major McAndrew, "what would your next step be?"

"Oh," said Emma. She hadn't thought this far. "I'd — I'd have to find the right people — I suppose I'd ask Daddy to tell me — people to make a thorough study of the creatures in a way that was safe for them. I mean, well, anybody you asked — *the* absolutely top people in their own fields — they'd come if they knew. I'm sure they would. You've got answers to a hundred riddles there about the dinosaurs —"

"Not dinosaurs," said Major McAndrew. "To judge by Andy's descriptions, we are discussing an extremely degenerate form of plesiosaur. It is, however, much the same thing."

"Aren't you . . . aren't you even going to go and look?" said Emma.

Major McAndrew shook his head.

"There is a danger that I might become interested," he said. "I am old. I cannot expect to finish more than one or two more jobs in my life. Πάντων χρημάτων ἄνθρωπον μέτρον εἶναι. That means Man is the measure of all things — Protagoras said it in the fifth century B.C., some time ago but the blink of an eyelid in the life of *your* creatures, Cousin Emma. But I believe it. If I can help solve some boring problem about the behavior of pests of the cocoa bean, I shall have done something. Marginally I may even have helped to prevent the species Homo sapiens from becoming extinct. I have wasted over fifty years — shut up, Roddy, I don't count the first eighteen — of a fair brain in a healthy body. I am going to judge this dilemma from a strictly selfish standpoint. My family will tell you that that is how I judge everything. But here it is because I can afford to waste no more of my life. So, first, I will vote with Cousin Emma, against Roddy and Andy, in the matter of the commercial exploitation of the cave. That produces a tied vote, two a side. As chairman of the meeting I am entitled to a casting vote, which I again cast against such exploitation. The peripheral matter of the tolerability of tourists is thus irrelevant. Now we come to the second question, the scientific exploitation of these creatures, in which I am going to vote against Cousin Emma, thus producing another tied vote. As chairman of the meeting —"

"On a point of order," said Andy.

Major McAndrew nodded solemnly.

"Is there anything in the rules," said Andy, "which excludes members who have been outvoted on the first motion from casting their votes on the second?"

"Nothing," said Major McAndrew. "I was just trying to pull a fast one. How do you vote, Andy and Roddy?"

"For the motion," said Andy.

"Against," said Roddy. "I don't see why we should have a load of boffins nosing around on our land if we're not going to make anything out of it."

"So be it," said Major McAndrew. "We still have a split vote, so as chairman I cast my vote against the motion."

"Notice how Father's got himself four votes," said Finn. "The Swiss haven't made him any less slippery."

"Cousin Emma appears dissatisfied," said Major McAndrew.

Emma bit her lip, fidgeted with her glass, and opened her mouth. The words wouldn't come. She took a sip of wine and tried again. They all waited for her.

"I can't understand you," she said, almost in a whisper. "Here's something terribly important and you treat it as a game. I *know* there are more important things, but they don't make this into — into a *joke*. I think I shall have to go. I'm sorry, but I shall have to go."

"A resignation!" said Roddy. "We've never had one of those before."

"Father's good as resigned," said Finn. "Only now and then he comes back and casts four votes."

"I hope you won't go, Cousin Emma," said Major McAndrew.

"Oh please not!" cried Miss Newcombe. "Emma's the only person who . . . oh, nothing. But please can she stay and do . . . whatever she was going to do . . . here?"

"Let me explain about the game," said Major McAndrew. "We are, as I believe you have discovered, a somewhat quarrelsome family. But we have survived. Like your creatures, we have adapted, and our adaptation has been to discuss all matters of any importance in this fashion, simply because it makes it much harder to quarrel if you have to quarrel through the chair. Now perhaps you will tell us what you propose to do, supposing you do leave us."

"I must write to my father and tell him everything that has happened. I'd ask him what to do next. He knows a lot of scientists. He might be able to think of a way of telling the right ones without letting the story out. Once they *knew* — Oh, I know it's your hill, your loch, your cave. But suppose one of *your* questions — about your beetles — suppose the answer to it lay in the territory of some chief who wouldn't let you come in — Daddy used to have that sort of trouble about tsetse flies — wouldn't you get there somehow and find the answer? Wouldn't that be what mattered?"

"At least she's addressing her remarks to the chair," said Roddy.

"Order," said Major McAndrew. "Yes, Cousin Emma, I would. In the past I have done exactly that sort of thing. I have lived among people like a friend and sent their secrets to other people, for what seemed to me at the time the greater good. I know now that it was a much less important matter than my boring doings with beetles, though I be-

201

lieve it to have been more important than Emma's plesio-saurs. Man is the measure of all things. You present us with a problem, Cousin Emma. In the past we could simply have done away with you, as an inconvenience, but now . . . now Poop won't let us."

"Certainly not!" said Miss Newcombe.

"On the other hand, I *can* write to your father and make out quite a good case that you have allowed yourself to be deluded by my children's persistent use of wild fantasy into inventing your own fantasy and pretending it was real."

"I can write to him too," said Finn, "explaining what a liar my father is."

"He'd believe *me*," said Emma. "At least — at least he wouldn't not believe me till he'd come up here to check."

"I think that is probably true. I suspect he might believe you without checking. So now it is clear that we have to *persuade* you to change your mind. First I will advance two arguments. There is a danger that your group of scientists, however careful, would themselves infect the creatures with some new bacteria, or otherwise imbalance their ecol-ogy. That may seem a remote risk, but this is not: you have fallen into the trap of judging all scientists by your father — selfless investigators interested only in expanding the field of human knowledge or in bettering the lot of their fellow men. But scientists, especially scientists of the cali-ber you would attract to a job like this, are different. Sci-ence itself is caught in a trap. In order to attract funds for his work the scientists must publish his findings, publish them before anyone else does. If he is an ambitious scien-tist, the need is even greater. Last year I read that an astronomer had detected minute traces of carbon monox-ide in one area of the heavens. No doubt this was impor-

202

tant, but was it important enough to justify his sending a telegram to every observatory in the world engaged in similar work? It struck me at the time that a postcard would have done. But that is how it is. Two men chance on the same drug on different sides of the world; it is the one who gets his discovery into print first who receives the Nobel Prize for medicine. There is thus no hope, no hope at all, that your group would keep their find secret. I am not now pulling a fast one. This is the world I know. And after publication, how long before Andy's commercial exploitation sets in? Five years? Ten? Even Protagoras would sneer."

"But if nobody knows . . ." muttered Emma, caught in the whirlpool of doubt.

"Yes. The question is whether it is better for your creature to subsist in its own strange way, unknown. Or whether it is better to have it thoroughly studied, and probably in the process kill it dead. It would then be *known;* you could find accounts of it in libraries, casts and skeletons in natural history museums. But it would be extinct, as the dodo is, and the oryx and the tiger almost are. Are you prepared to choose, Cousin Emma? No? Then I am going to help you by casting another vote."

"Five?" said Finn.

"It isn't a record," said Andy. "He cast eight one evening when Mother was staying."

"Not my vote," said Major McAndrew and rose carefully from his chair. As soon as he was out of the room Roddy gave a long whistle.

"Wow!" he said. "I've never seen him as nearly cornered as that. My hat, Cousin Emma, I thought you'd got him. He as good as told us he really was a spy, and he's never let on about that before."

"Who's he gone to fetch, though?" said Finn. "Mary?"

"He could have rung for her," said Andy. "I bet it's Andy Coaches. Andy Coaches is the rightful Chief, but his grandfather got drunk at the Clan Gathering of 1862 and wore his sporran upside-down, so he was deprived of the chieftainship, which his descendants can only resume in times of unprecedented danger."

Emma sat in a sort of trance, not noticing how much her throat was hurting again after all the talking. All she wished was that it had been someone else who'd sat in *Anadyomene*, who was now sitting in her chair. She looked across to where Miss Newcombe was making faces at herself in a spoon and wondered if it would have been any easier if the creature had been as beautiful as that — beautiful like the Arabian oryx, or even beautiful and dangerous like the tiger — instead of being a living nightmare out of old time. Vermin, Roddy had said. Suppose it were rats. Suppose some disease almost wiped out the rats of the world, and there was only a small colony left on one island. . . .

Roddy and Finn were compiling a list of the disgraceful items that had fallen out of Andy Coaches' grandfather's upside-down sporran when Major McAndrew returned. In one hand he carried two dark gray books; Emma knew them at once by the ripple pattern on the edges of the paper. In his other hand he carried a long skull; Emma knew that too, by the ragged teeth. When he sat down and put the three objects in front of him, Emma saw that the skull had an irregular white star between the eyeholes, a place where something had smashed through the bone and the hole had later been mended with plaster of Paris.

"I propose to cast my father's vote," said Major McAndrew. "Your great-grandfather's, Cousin Emma. When he died and I inherited, one of the things I inherited was the safe in the laboratory. That had always puzzled me, as he had never let me see inside it although he was a very careless man about his personal possessions. For instance, he endured for many years a valet who stole and stole, simply because the man was able to polish my father's boots to the standard he expected. So I had been unable to imagine what he wanted to lock up. In fact, I found very little in the safe. A number of formulae and descriptions of inventions of possible commercial value. A number of letters from a woman — not my mother. These books and this skull. The skull has been shot with a heavy-caliber bullet, such as he used for big game; you can still just read the date he wrote on it, September 8, 1890. The books are my father's diaries for 1889 and 1890, but many of the pages are missing. They have simply been torn out. For instance, though he describes the building of *Anadyomene* in some detail, he removed the pages saying why he decided to build her. There is even one page missing in the middle of his account of her workings, which must have been to do with the electrical system."

"He didn't want anyone to know he was going to use her at night," said Emma. "He probably wrote more about putting in a searchlight than he would have if he'd just wanted her for daytime. He must have heard the wildcats calling at night and somehow realized that they weren't."

"The echo!" said Andy. "Big House was burned in 1887, so he won't have started to sleep down here till after that. *I've* sometimes thought those calls were coming from the middle of the loch!"

"And so have I," said Major McAndrew. "We live and learn. I think it is safe to deduce that he found his way into the cave, shot his specimen, and then came to many of the same conclusions that Cousin Emma has about the likelihood of the creature's survival if exposed to the full impact of Victorian inquisitiveness. He was a remarkable man in many ways. I wish I had liked him more. Be that as it may, he locked the skull away and, to make doubly sure, destroyed the relevant material in his diary. I have always known there was some sort of a creature in the loch, because of the skull."

"That's why you backed Mary up about us not swimming much!" said Finn.

"Certainly I decided that it would be unwise to cross any of the local superstitions about the loch."

"And he put a stopper on the other entrance," said Roddy. "Darwin's Pimple."

"I wonder how he killed it," said Andy. "Not easy, with only one other person in Anna. It would have to be in the dark, and then he'd have to hack the skull off somehow — he couldn't have got the whole body into Anna."

"I bet the other ones ate what he left," said Roddy. "They have that sort of mean look, which people do have who eat their relations."

He gnashed his teeth convincingly at Finn, but it only reminded Emma how much there was still to know, how little they'd been able to discover in their brief plunge into the dark abysm. Did they eat their dead? What did they do with the bones? Drop them instinctively in the gulf? How . . .

"Well, Cousin Emma," said Andy. "Has the old tempter changed your mind? I must say I'm going to start looking for a girl who has an overwhelming tendency to agree with everything I say, and hope that some of that factor is inherited by the kids. Then I shan't have any of this split-vote trouble. We'll raise a little brood of yes-men."

"It's interesting that Emma's grandmother was the only one who had the nerve to say no to Grandfather," said Finn. "Some of *that* factor's been transmitted."

"Well, Cousin Emma?" said Major McAndrew.

"I don't know. If *he* — Can we go to bed? I might know what I think in the morning."

10

*Emma was burning her diary. Then, at least,
she would be able to start learning to pretend that
none of it had ever happened.*

She knelt by the grate holding each sheet carefully horizontal so that the line of flame moved very slowly across it,
only a little yellow at the peaks but a beautiful intense blue
where the flame met the paper. The blue was curved like a
liquid, like a blue wave, and under it the paper was red for
half an inch before it fissured, curled, turned black and
dropped in the grate. When each sheet was down to a little
triangle of white around her thumb she let it fall; the wide
margins she had left meant that there was no writing on
the triangle. Then she read the next sheet carefully
through, lit another match (which was extravagant,

but . . .) and started the march of flame at the top left-hand corner.

Once a tear fell on the middle of a sheet, blotching the firm curves of a word, making them hairy and fuzzy. When the flames reached that place they sidled round it and joined up again where the paper was dry, so that when she let the final corner of that sheet fall there was a different-shaped piece of unburned paper already lying in the hearth; it had the shape of a creature, but not *the* creature — more like the elephant Babar with floppy wings. Emma turned the piece over to see what the one word saved had been: it was part of "although" — no comfort at all. But it wouldn't betray anything, either.

As she was burning page eight the flame wavered as if the draft had changed, and then recovered. When she let that corner fall a voice above her head said "What are you doing, Emma?"

She scrambled up, almost knocking Major McAndrew over; he moved fussily away.

"I smelled burning," he said. "You are dressed very early. But old men are allowed to get up and wander round their houses in the dawn."

"I always get up early. I've been writing a diary, but now I decided I ought to burn it. It was all about . . ."

She nodded her head towards the loch, gray on a gray day, neither storm nor sun. It, too, was betraying nothing.

"May I see?" he said.

She clicked the hoops together and passed him the folder; he sat on the bed and began to read. After a couple of lines he looked up and said "Nice writing — I don't need my glasses." Then he read on, page after page, slowly, as though he were studying a book in a language he knew fairly well but hadn't read for some time. He never changed his position, never said anything at all. At first Emma stood by the fireplace, moving from foot to foot and wondering what he was thinking. Later she sat down on the stool by her dressing table, got out her mending kit, and sewed a patch onto the tear in her spare jeans, which she'd ripped yesterday, sailing with Finn and Roddy. She sewed slowly and badly, but she'd almost finished when she heard him put the folder down.

"You mustn't burn that," he said.

"I thought I ought to. Your father did."

"Old people aren't always right. When Andy accused you of nearly drowning Poop, you didn't say anything about my children nearly killing you two or three times."

"It didn't matter."

"Um. Roddy seems to have behaved quite well in the cave."

"He wouldn't give up. He must have been just as tired and frightened as I was, but he wouldn't be beaten."

"But it was you who had to go back with Andy."

"That's not Roddy's fault! He's just like that!"

"So am I. I have to get air hostesses to help me down the steps from airplanes. They think it's because they're beautiful, but in fact it's because I'm frightened."

He picked up the diary again and began to leaf back and forth through it as though he were looking for the best bits to reread. Emma stood there for a while, hoping.

"Do you mean I can take it back to school?" she said at last.

"No," he said. "No, I don't think you can do that. But I'll put it in the safe with the skull."

He looked at her, then suddenly put up his hand as if he

were trying to remove the spectacles he hadn't been using.

"That's not good enough?" he asked.

Emma explained about Sarah Davidson and the School Prize. Major McAndrew got up while she was talking and looked out of the window. When she finished he laughed.

"There's never enough to do in the mornings," he said. "My beetles are too boring, even to me, for me to work on them more than a few hours a day. We'll spend these early hours together, faking the record."

"Oh," said Emma. "Is that fair? I mean — I mean one of the things about my diary when we were *inventing* a creature was that — that I'd got the truth written down. Even if no one except a few teachers ever read it."

"My dear Cousin Emma — I apologize — I must learn to call you Emma, and I wonder if you're right about the effect of calling Poop Poop — where was I? Yes, you've *got* to fake a diary, or you will go back to school without one. I do not propose that it should contain any lies. I've had an odd life, and wasted most of it, but I've seen more places and people than twenty worthier citizens. For instance, I take it that these teachers of yours are interested in poetry. Would the name T. S. Eliot impress them?"

"Oh, yes!"

"I knew Tom Eliot pretty well at one time. Not only can I tell you about jaunts and jollities with him, but I've got a manuscript of his somewhere, an early draft of *The Coming of the Magi,* with lines in it that aren't in the printed version. We could take a photostat of that and stick it in — do you think that might score a few marks?"

"Oh, yes!"

"Then there's nature — flora and fauna. I've always been too lazy to produce a proper catalogue of the plants in this valley, but some of them are pretty rare, and I think I can definitely disprove all the current theories about the revegetation of western Scotland after the Ice Ages. I ought to have written it up into a paper years ago, but now you can do it instead."

"Are you sure," said Emma, "that your plants don't prove that the valley was never properly iced over because of the hot springs?"

"Ah," he said. "Yes, there's that. What a mercy I never wrote that paper. Never mind, we've plenty of fauna which are almost as interesting. I'll try and show you a golden eagle."

"Can we start now?"

"I don't see why not — there's forty minutes till breakfast. Let's start with the day Goering tried to hire me to assassinate Churchill. We'll invent a picnic, during which I hold all hearers enthralled with this absurd misunderstanding; that means that on the way up we'll have been able to watch a pine marten — there aren't many of them left now. Don't look at me like that, Cous— like that, Emma. I'll show you a pine marten this evening, to make it true. Are you ready? Right. 'Today we went up Ben Goig for a picnic. The hills were all brown, with mauve shadows in the clefts and folds —' "

"I can put in those bits," said Emma rather stiffly.

"Please," she added.

J
F
DIC

Dickinson, Peter

Emma Tupper s diary

DATE			